"For God's sake, Jane, I'm not talking about love."

Jane responded bluntly. "Oh? What are you talking about, Blake? Just good old plain unvarnished sex?"

"No," Blake murmured. "I'm not talking about sex, not the way you mean. I like you, Jane. I like being with you. I also find you very attractive physically. Is there something wrong with that?"

"Me!" Jane laughed. "Listen, Blake, I've been plain-Jane all my life. After the beautiful women you've known, I'm just a novelty to you. There's nothing remotely glamorous or sexy about me, and we both know it."

"No," he said slowly. "you're not glamorous, but whoever told you that you weren't sexy was either out of his mind or senile or blind."

Rosemary Hammond lives on the West Coast but has traveled extensively through the United States, Mexico and Canada with her husband. She loves to write and has been fascinated by the mechanics of fiction ever since her college days. She reads extensively, enjoying everything from Victorian novels to mysteries, spy stories and, of course, romances.

Books by Rosemary Hammond

HARLEQUIN ROMANCE
2601—FULL CIRCLE
2655—TWO DOZEN RED ROSES
2674—THE SCENT OF HIBISCUS

HARLEQUIN PRESENTS
802—THE HABIT OF LOVING
859—MALIBU MUSIC
896—LOSER TAKE ALL

These books may be available at your local bookseller.

Don't miss any of our special offers. Write to us at the following address for information on our newest releases.

Harlequin Reader Service
901 Fuhrmann Blvd., P.O. Box 1397, Buffalo, NY 14240
Canadian address: P.O. Box 603,
Fort Erie, Ont. L2A 5X3

Plain Jane
Rosemary Hammond

Harlequin Books

TORONTO • NEW YORK • LONDON
AMSTERDAM • PARIS • SYDNEY • HAMBURG
STOCKHOLM • ATHENS • TOKYO • MILAN

Original hardcover edition published in 1986
by Mills & Boon Limited

ISBN 0-373-02817-2

Harlequin Romance first edition February 1987

CHAPTER ONE

JANE stood at her desk staring down at next month's garden layout, trying to decide whether to feature forsythia or lilac in the one full-colour page she was allowed by the managing editor of *Northwest Life Magazine*. It was always an agonising decision. She could have filled a hundred pages with the seemingly endless bounty of blooming plants that filled Northwest gardens with blazing colour in the spring, and she always had trouble making the crucial choice.

She was finding it especially difficult to concentrate today. A new building was going up right next door, creeping slowly upward until it was now directly opposite Jane's office, and the noise was deafening, both from the sounds of the construction workers busy at their labours and the explicit and highly appreciative comments of her three office mates, their admiring audience.

It was also Fat Tuesday in Seattle, and she had promised Randi and Jennifer and Stephanie she'd go down to Pioneer Square with them after work to join in the festivities. Ordinarily, she would have ignored the whole affair as a little too wild and exuberant for her quieter tastes, but the three models who shared her work space with her had insisted, and she liked them all so much that she had finally given in.

Now, of course, she was sorry. The whole venture made her nervous. She wasn't fond of crowds or noise, and she knew there would be plenty of both, so that between her apprehension over the coming evening and the pounding and drilling and sawing going on next door, she gave the colour photographs spread out on her desk a last rueful look and admitted defeat.

She put the pictures back in their folder and pushed it aside. Leaning back in her chair, she glanced at the three models who were clustered at the window, deeply engrossed in what was going on across the way. Jane smiled as she listened to them.

'Ooh, look at that one,' squealed Jennifer. 'What a bod!'

'I like the hunk in the red shirt,' crooned Stephanie. 'But preferably without the shirt. Look at those lovely bulges.'

'Where are you looking, dear?' Randi asked archly.

All three girls burst into a fit of the giggles then. With a sigh, Jane decided she might as well give up and go and see what it was that they all found so captivating. It wasn't coming right, anyway. A break might do her good. She gave the empty mock-up spread out on her worktable one last rueful glance and walked over to join the others at the window.

They were so intent on the building next door that when she came up behind them, they didn't even notice her. Jane realised that she was that kind of person anyway. People tended to overlook her, no matter what the occasion. She was used to it by now, though, and had long since come to terms with the fact that she would never turn heads with her neat conservative clothes, simple short hairstyle and normal, unexciting features.

It wasn't that she had ever lacked for dates, even

admirers, but the men who took her out seemed to be more interested in her mind, her work, her good sense, even her friendly advice, than they were in her face or figure. Actually, this suited her. She wouldn't know how to handle being the centre of attention, like the three models. Besides, she reassured herself again, there was always Robert, and, as her mother had pointed out long ago, plain was definitely better than ugly.

She stood behind Jennifer and Randi now. Both of them were taller than she was, but there was just enough space between the long auburn curls and the sleek golden mane to give her a clear view of the building site.

It had been under construction for months, almost a year, if you counted the demolition of the previous block of run-down shops, seedy office building and small hotel that used to be there. It seemed to Jane that these days, on every street corner in Seattle, a building was either being torn down or constructed, changing the skyline of the city so dramatically and quickly that a person who only came into town once a year wouldn't even recognise it.

The building had progressed now to the point where they were working on the twentieth floor, directly opposite the workroom at eye level, and Jane wondered if there would even be a fashion section in the next few issues of *Northwest Life* unless the managing editor put blinkers on the models or tied them up or moved them to the other side of the building.

As she stood there and watched all the interesting masculine activity, however, Jane had to admit that she could understand the attraction. The whole area seemed to be filled with strong muscular men in various states of dress and undress. For the past few days, Seattle had been enjoying an unseasonably warm, dry spell of weather, and the workmen had shed their heavy winter jackets, even, in some cases, their shirts. It would be murder, Jane thought, if they didn't complete the twentieth floor before summer and proceed upwards with their labours. If a mildly warm day in March could strip them down to their undershirts, what would August bring?

Although she knew the men were all supposed to wear hard hats, she noticed that most of them had taken them off and that many heads of hair were conspicuously well-combed. It was clear, too, that a lot of the bustle and activity going on next door was conducted primarily with the end in view of impressing their admiring audience. Surely, Jane thought, men concentrating solely on their work didn't normally pose and strut that way every time they lifted a board or hammered a nail.

It reminded her of her high-school days, when the boys would congregate together to play ball and studiously ignore the girls passing by, while at the same time running a little faster or leaping a little higher just to put on a show of masculine strength.

'Well, Jane, what do you make of all this?' asked Randi Tatum in an amused tone.

Jane smiled at the tall honey-blonde. Randi was the magazine's fashion editor, and the two of them, with full responsibility for their respective departments, had developed a splendid working relationship over the past two years. Quite an achievement, Jane often thought, considering how different they were in every conceivable respect.

'I think it's a very, um, entertaining spectacle,'

Jane said to her now. 'Makes it hard to concentrate on spring flowering shrubs for Northwest gardens, however.'

A shrill whistle blew just then, and immediately all activity ceased. It was obviously clocking off time. With friendly waves at the girls, the men started shrugging into their shirts and jackets, picked up their lunch boxes, and swarmed towards the lift.

'See anything you like?' Stephanie asked Jane.

Jane smiled. 'How could I possibly choose among such goodies?' she said good-naturedly. She shook her head. 'And I thought it was hard to decide between forsythia and lilac.'

'Oh, Jane's not really interested in those macho types,' Jennifer put in. 'She's got Robert.'

The remark was meant to be kindly, Jane knew. Lovely, auburn-haired Jennifer didn't have a mean bone in her body. She just wasn't too bright.

'Yes,' Jane agreed, 'there's always Robert.'

Stephanie and Jennifer turned to leave, then, for their next appointment, promising to return at five o'clock for their excursion to Pioneer Square. When they were gone, Randi turned to Jane.

'How is Robert?' she asked.

Jane looked at her in surprise. 'He's fine. Same as always. Why do you ask?'

The tall blonde shrugged. 'I don't know. I thought I detected a marked lack of enthusiasm in your voice when you spoke of him just now.'

Jane laughed. 'Oh, Randi, you should know by now that I'm not the enthusiastic type. I couldn't handle all the excitement you three glamour girls generate.'

Randi shook her head slowly from side to side. 'Sometimes I wonder if you're for real, Jane.'

'Why?'

'You're so determined to convince everybody, yourself included, that you're some kind of dull mouse.'

Jane grinned. 'Well, I just face the facts, ma'am. Besides, I'm not complaining. I'm satisfied with myself and my life just the way they are.'

'That's what worries me,' Randi said tartly.

Suddenly she grabbed Jane by the arm and turned her slightly so that they both faced the full-length mirror put up on one wall for the benefit of the models. Jane had to smile at the contrast between the two of them. Randi was a good six inches taller in her high heels, but it was far more than that.

Randi held herself with the confidence of a woman who was supremely aware of her attributes. Her make-up was a work of art, her smooth golden hair sprayed to shining perfection, and her black dress hugged her figure in all the right places.

'Now,' Randi said firmly, 'what do you see?'

Very seriously, Jane studied both their reflections for several seconds, then, straight-faced, she turned and looked up at Randi.

'I see a glamour girl and a mouse,' she said with mock solemnity.

'Now, be serious,' Randi snapped. 'Forget me. Just look at yourself and tell me what you see.'

'All right.' She gazed at herself again in the mirror, then said, 'I see a medium tall, rather slim, pleasant-looking woman of twenty-six who is not, has never been, will never be, a head-turner.'

'Do you know what I see?' Randi asked.

'No, but I'm sure you're going to tell me.'

'I see potential.'

'Potential?'

Randi nodded. 'Look at you. You've got all that wonderful shiny thick hair. It's just the wrong colour. You have marvellous bones, but you don't know beans about make-up. You've got a near-perfect figure, but dress like a—like a . . .'

'A middle-aged frump?' Jane put in helpfully.

'No, a lady lawyer. You know, trying to be one of the boys. They all look alike with their little tailored suits and mannish shirts and little ties.' She rolled her eyes. 'And the shoes!'

'You've just given a perfect description of my entire wardrobe,' Jane said drily.

'That's what I'm trying to tell you!' Randi wailed. 'Put yourself in my hands, and I'll make you glamorous in one day.'

Jane put a hand lightly on Randi's arm. 'Listen, Randi, I know you mean well, and I appreciate your concern, really I do. But glamour isn't only a matter of clothes and make-up, it's a state of mind, an attitude. I don't *think* like a glamour girl. I don't *feel* like one and, to tell you the honest truth, I really don't want to be one. Honestly, Randi, I mean it.'

Randi sighed deeply. 'OK, kiddo, if you say so. But if you ever change your mind, you come to Mama Tatum, and I'll transform you. You should have seen Jennifer when she first came to me. From a caterpillar to a butterfly overnight.'

Jane laughed. 'You're a miracle worker, I know, but you'd be wasting your time on me.'

'All right, but you are coming with us tonight. You're not going to back out at the last minute because your petunias need pruning or something.'

'It's too early for petunias, and you don't prune them, but yes, I'm coming. Everyone should go to one Fat Tuesday, I suppose, just for the experience.'

Fat Tuesday, the pre-Lenten celebration that drew musicians and revellers down to Pioneer Square on the waterfront of Puget Sound like a magnet, is a literal translation of the French 'Mardi Gras' and Seattle's version of that traditional New Orleans holiday. For the whole week preceding Ash Wednesday, nightly events were scheduled—band concerts, open houses, free entertainment, colourful pavement displays—culminating in a grand free-for-all on Tuesday night, with a torchlight parade and a street dance.

The sky had clouded over suddenly in the late afternoon, and by the time the four girls got off the crowded bus at First and Washington in the heart of the Square, it was raining steadily. Seattle natives learn young, however, that if they wait until the sun shines to go on the picnic or boat trip or to the football game, they never go out at all, and both Randi and Jane had come equipped with umbrellas.

The wet narrow streets were already crowded with people, not all of them sober, and it was getting dark. There was every variety of participant and spectator, office workers, teenagers, young couples with children, old people, and many of them wore outlandish costumes with garish masks. Several impromptu street bands were blaring, there were food stalls on the pavements, and, down at the end of the street, the informal, makeshift parade was beginning to form.

Jane followed along after her three companions, completely out of her element in all the noise and confusion. It was so loud, she thought, as she walked along balancing her umbrella and trying not to get her feet wet in the puddles that had collected on the pavement. There was a lot of good-natured shouting and singing. Several people carried drinks in their hands, and twice she was almost shoved off the pavement into the street.

They finally arrived at the French restaurant where they had decided to have dinner. Randi led the way inside, where it was a little quieter, but barely. At least it was dry, Jane thought gratefully, as she shook out her umbrella in the small foyer.

All the tables in the dining-room seemed to be occupied, so they decided to have a drink in the cocktail lounge while they waited. Jane could take liquor or leave it alone, but tonight, wet and cold, stunned by all the confusion, a drink sounded like a very good idea. Besides, she thought, as she followed the tall blonde Randi into the bar, it might help her enter into a more festive spirit.

It was really hard not to. In the next second, a strange young man seized her around the waist and kissed her soundly on the mouth. Startled, she drew back, half-wondering if she should call for help. Then she looked around and saw that the statuesque Randi was receiving a similar demonstration of uninhibited affection from a perfect stranger, and, what's more, seemed to be enjoying it. The young man who had kissed her only laughed at the surprised look on her face, then moved on to Jennifer. Jane smiled back at him and waved.

Miraculously, they found a tiny table in the far corner of the room and sat down. They had a round of drinks, then another, and by the time they had been served their third drink, Jane was feeling light-headed and very hungry. She was about to suggest they try again for the dining-room, when a large woman knocked against their wobbly little table, spilling her drink directly into Jane's lap.

Jane mopped it up with the minuscule bar napkin as best she could. When she'd finished, she looked up to see the other girls disappearing on to a tiny dance floor. At the same moment, the volume was turned up, and a blast of loud rock music blared into the room.

Jane sat there alone at the table wondering whether she should go and join them or try to find some food on her own or simply go home. She stood up, wobbling a little uncertainly. Her feet were wet, her stomach was empty, her head was pounding, and she couldn't even think straight over the racket that assaulted her ears.

She thought with longing of her safe little house on Mercer Island, but, before she tried to drive home, the first thing she'd better do was to get out of there and try to find a cracker or some peanuts to nibble on, anything to give her a little nourishment.

This is not my cup of tea, she thought grimly as a strong wave of dizziness passed over her the minute she stood up. No more trying to be a good sport. A sudden spasm of nausea gripped her, a cold perspiration broke out on her forehead, and a sudden blackness appeared behind her eyes. Hanging on to the backs of chairs for support, she began to edge her way through the crowd out of the bar and towards the front entrance.

Once out on the pavement, the fresh air helped to clear her head a little, but she still felt unsteady on her feet. The crowds outside only seemed to have grown worse than before, and the noise was deafening. Her head was still spinning, and as she felt herself being carried along by the surging hordes of people, she began to panic. She felt really ill now, her empty stomach heaving from the unaccustomed liquor and her knees buckling under her so that all that held her upright were the other bodies pressed up against her, pushing her.

Finally, she knew that in the next instant she would simply pass out, disgrace herself, possibly even be trampled in the street. As she closed her eyes and felt herself slip towards unconsciousness, she had a fleeting vision of tomorrow's headlines: 'Garden Editor of *Northwest Life Magazine* Drunk in Streets.' She groaned aloud at the thought.

Just as she was about to fall, she came up against a solid object. She felt a strong arm come around her, pulling her out of the crowd and into a doorway. With a sob of relief, she slumped up against a broad chest, totally thoughtless and uncaring who or what her sudden saviour might be, but merely infinitely grateful. Whatever this new development brought, she decided weakly, it had to be better than fainting in the street.

Little by little, the waves of dizziness subsided, and her stomach began to settle down. The inside of her head was still decidedly fuzzy, but with the welcome support of those strong arms to reassure her, she closed her eyes and let out a deep sigh of relief.

'Don't be frightened,' she heard a masculine voice say just above her.

For the first time it dawned on her that this haven of security she'd stumbled upon so gratefully was actually a person instead of a disembodied pair of arms. A man, to boot. She opened her eyes and looked up. It was a man, all right.

He was quite tall, and she could see by the glare of the torches out in the street flickering over his face that he was very attractive, possibly the most attractive man she'd ever seen. He seemed to be smiling, but her mind was still not functioning properly and the light was so dim that she couldn't really tell.

'Are you all right now?' she heard him ask.

She could only nod. He had a pleasant voice, low-pitched and not at all threatening. She had a fleeting vision of a finely sculptured mouth as he spoke. He was clean-shaven and he smelled of soap and fresh linen.

'What happened to you?' he asked. 'Are you ill? Do you need a doctor?'

He had pulled a little away from her. His hands were still on her shoulders, and he was staring down at her. She wished she could see him more clearly. She began to feel a faint stirring of alarm. He seemed all right, clean, well-spoken, but she could think of at least two serial rapists now on trial in Seattle, both of whom were eminently presentable, even quite good-looking.

'I think,' she said, striving for a precise tone, 'that I am a little drunk.' She was astonished to hear how slurred her words came out.

He laughed then, a low chuckle deep in his throat, and let her go. As his hands left her shoulders, she felt an odd mixture of relief and disappointment and, along with it, a sudden inexplicable surge of longing.

It was oddly exciting to be alone with a strange man in a strange place, the crowds milling about just a few feet away, and the drinks she'd had on an empty stomach had released her normal inhibitions just enough to make the situation seem not only unthreatening, but very interesting, even romantic.

It was all so unlike her, she thought briefly, with her solid, sensible approach to life. It was as though a side of her that had lain dormant, that she had even actively repressed for as long as she could remember, was suddenly emerging.

She looked up at him. Really, she thought, he's very handsome. He was dark, with thick black hair cut rather long. His face was long, with a square chin, a strong nose, and deep indentations running along his cheeks when he smiled that were not quite dimples.

They were standing very close still, not quite touching, when suddenly a rowdy group of passers-by jostled against her, pushing her off balance so that she fell against him, and once again his arms came around her. She had a sudden insane desire to press her cheek against his, to touch his hair, his face, to feel his mouth on hers.

Then she heard someone calling her name. She recognised Randi's voice, and immediately came to her senses. She pulled back from him and felt his hands drop away.

'I hear my friends calling me,' she said. 'Thank you so much for rescuing me. I was really quite frightened.'

He inclined his head. 'Not at all. Glad to have been of service. Are you sure you're all right now?'

'Oh, yes. Quite sure.'

She turned round and caught a brief glimpse of Randi's blonde head. She waved and called to her, then turned back to thank the stranger again. But he was gone. She looked up the street and could barely make out a tall, broad-shouldered man with dark hair moving away from her through the crowd.

Feeling more disappointed, even bereft, than she would have thought possible from such a brief encounter, she started pushing through the people towards Randi. The parade was over now and the crowd thinning out. Her dizzy spell was gone. They would get something to eat, then she would drive home and resume her normal everyday life again.

That's what she wanted, what she had worked so hard to achieve. A nice, sane, sensible life, where you accepted the cards fate had dealt you and didn't go mooning off on a futile quest for the impossible.

Safe in her little house on Mercer Island at last, sober, fed and very tired from the traumatic evening, Jane thought once again about the stranger. It was nothing, she told herself for the tenth time as she brushed her teeth. Absolutely nothing.

She rinsed her mouth out and stared into the mirror over the bathroom sink, thinking perhaps she had been transformed in some magical way by that chance encounter.

But it was the same old Jane. Plain Jane, she thought, regretting once again the sentimentality of the mother who had named her after her favourite writer. To be so plain and to be saddled with such a name, even in honour of the wonderful Miss Austen, was really too much.

There had been times when she was growing up when she'd almost wished she'd been born downright ugly, with a hooked nose or squint eyes instead of this awful drabness.

'But, darling,' she could remember her mother saying to her in one of her bouts of depression, 'you have so many good qualities. Be grateful you're not homely. You have nice regular features, beautiful skin and really lovely brown hair.'

There's nothing really *wrong* with my looks, she thought again, but nothing right, either, and all those good features still add up to dull, dull, dull. If only her mother had given her a glamorous name, she thought. Delilah. Rozanne. Rosalind. But Jane!

She thought again about the man who had rescued her tonight and how he had let her go without demur the minute she had pulled away from him. Not that she'd actually wanted him to kiss her or hold her or spirit her away for a romantic intrigue, but still, it would have been nice, just for once, to have been viewed by a devastating man like that as a sex object, to have at least experienced the pleasure of being *asked*.

She got into bed and switched off the light. It was still raining, and she lay in bed staring up at the ceiling in the dark and listening to the pattering on the roof.

If it had been statuesque Randi, she thought, or dark, mysterious Stephanie, or vibrant, red-headed Jennifer, the story would have had a different ending altogether. Instead, he'd got plain Jane, the 'nice' girl with all the 'good' features, whom everybody liked, but who would never set any man on fire.

'Now stop that!' she said aloud into the silent room.

Then she had to laugh. She'd been through it all

before and would probably go through it all again. There were worse things in life than being plain and unexciting.

Think of Robert, she told herself. Nice, safe Robert, who cared about her for all the 'good' qualities she was treating with such contempt, and who would probably eventually want to marry her. Be grateful for what you can have, she admonished herself sternly.

She dutifully thought of Robert. He was nice-looking, he had a good job in a prominent law firm, he would make a wonderful husband, and she'd known him all her life. He was gentle, kind, considerate and never pushed her into lovemaking.

Yes, she thought, settling comfortably into the pillows and drawing the quilt up around her neck. Think of Robert. But as she drifted off into sleep, her last thought was of a tall dark stranger with strong arms, a broad chest, and a flashing smile.

By the next day, Jane's essentially practical nature had reasserted itself, and the embarrassing events of Fat Tuesday were fading into a dim memory. When she got to the office that morning, she had already made the firm decision that it was too late for forsythia. She would go with lilacs for the April issue.

She and Randi were supposed to share the long narrow workroom on the twentieth floor of the Cascade Building equally, but, in practice, the tall blonde and her two regular models had spread out to cover at least three-quarters of the available space with their belongings, leaving Jane with just enough room at one end for her worktable and stool. Jane didn't object. She liked all three girls very much and rather enjoyed their constant chatter about clothes, make-up, diets, hairstyles, and, of course, the most burning topic of all— MEN!

All three were quite lovely to look at as well. Tall, blonde Randi, with her polished sophisticated aura of glamour. The dusky, black-haired Stephanie, with her creamy complexion and mysterious eyes. Luscious Jennifer, with the cascade of auburn hair and her ebullient outgoing personality.

As usual, this morning all three of them were gathered at the window again, deeply engrossed in the entertainment offered by the construction workers next door. The hammering and drilling and sawing had come to seem like a normal part of the background by now, almost as familiar as the traffic noises on the busy street below.

Jane came up behind them on her way to her own section of the room, drawn almost against her will by curiosity as she listened to their comments.

'Oh, God,' Jennifer breathed. 'He looks like a Viking.'

'Or a Nordic god,' echoed Stephanie.

Across the way, Jane could see a very tall blond young man come walking towards them to the very edge of the floor. He was carrying a heavy load of steel girders, and his powerful muscles bulged impressively under his thin vest. He was grinning openly at the girls as he slowly lowered his load, and when he stood up, he assumed the Charles Atlas pose, flexing his powerful biceps for their benefit. The girls cracked up at that, and started screaming with laughter and bursting into appreciative applause.

Then, suddenly, the Viking froze. He slowly turned his head. In a split second, he dropped his pose and bent down to sort through the pile of girders. Jane noticed that all heads turned towards a tall man who had just stepped off the makeshift lift.

'Oh, oh,' she heard Randi murmur. 'Here comes Simon Legree.'

There was an immediate flurry of activity. All the hard hats were clapped on, and every man on the floor suddenly became very absorbed in his job. The newcomer strode purposefully over to the Viking and, glaring fiercely under heavy dark brows, raised an arm and pointed to a nearby pile of lumber, obviously issuing a very explicit order. Like a shot, the Viking turned to obey.

'He must be some kind of foreman or superintendent,' Jane said.

Randi laughed. 'He shows up at the most unexpected times and always catches them by surprise. They'll be having an absolutely marvellous time strutting around and putting on a show for us, but the minute he comes round, they really hop to it.'

Jane gazed curiously at the foreman. Why did he instil such fear in the men? He was no bigger than the others but, since most of them were giants, that still made him very tall. Although he didn't appear to be quite as muscle-bound as some of them, she saw him lift a piece of heavy machinery with apparent ease. It was hard to tell, anyway, because he was wearing a heavy woollen plaid shirt and a hard hat.

There was an air of command about him, though, she noticed, that seemed to make quite a deep impression on his subordinates, who were now studiously ignoring the windowful of admiring women next door. She noticed, too, that after one brief glance the foreman never once looked their way.

Such devotion to duty made her feel a little guilty about her own dereliction, and she decided she'd better get back to work herself. The models' enthusiasm seemed to be ebbing anyway, with the damper cast on their view by the newcomer, and the group was breaking up.

Before she turned away, Jane gave one last glance at the tall foreman. He was bending over a metal saw that seemed to be malfunctioning, and examining the wicked-looking blade carefully. He fiddled with a switch, tightened a bolt, and the saw whined briefly into life, then died again. He straightened up then and stared into space with a faintly puzzled expression on his face. He turned slightly in Jane's direction, giving her a clearer view of his face.

What a handsome man, she thought appreciatively, quite the best-looking man she'd seen since . . .

Then she drew in her breath sharply. Even at this distance, some twenty feet, she recognised him. It was her nameless rescuer from last night.

She stared, transfixed, as he took off the hard hat to run a hand over a thick head of very dark hair, cut rather long and curling around his ears. Then, holding the hat in one hand, he stood with his long legs apart, his hands at his sides, in a thoughtful pose. Jane dimly heard a telephone ringing in the background and the models' chattering as they got back to business, but all her attention was focused on the dark man across the way.

She felt oddly compelled to memorise his face, his tall straight figure, as she might a painting or a statue, so that she could carry it with her in her mind and take pleasure from it. There was nothing personal in this feeling. She didn't know him and was quite certain she never would. She didn't even want to know him. A man who looked like that would have to be vain, arrogant and totally spoiled by women. She only wanted to admire.

His face was long, with a straight nose, a rather square bony jaw, and a beautifully sculptured mouth, and the heavy dark brows and lean indented cheeks gave him a faint air of mystery. She could well understand, looking at him now, how he could command such respect from his men. He was just as she remembered him from last night when she'd run into him and he'd held her in his arms in the crowd down in Pioneer Square.

Then, suddenly, he looked her way, as though aware of her gaze on him. Their eyes met. She was briefly conscious of a dazzling flash of bright blue before she dropped her eyes and turned away, flushed and embarrassed, and slightly guilty at having been caught staring at him that way.

CHAPTER TWO

HE couldn't possibly have recognised her, she thought, as she turned away in confusion. It had been dark, their meeting had been brief, only lasting a matter of a few minutes, and she was well aware of the fact that she had a decidedly unmemorable face.

'Gorgeous, isn't he?' she heard Randi murmur beside her.

'Yes, he is,' Jane agreed quickly. Then she added with a smile, 'They all are.'

'Ah, but this one's special.'

'Do you know him?' Jane asked. She wouldn't be surprised. All three models seemed to have a long string of attractive men panting after them.

Randi sighed regretfully. 'Only his name, I'm afraid. I've run into him at a few parties and been introduced. He's Blake Bannister.'

Then Jane remembered the sign posted at the street level of the new building. Bannister Construction Company.

'I see,' she said with a raise of her eyebrows. 'The boss. No wonder they all scattered.' She paused, then said, 'I take it you don't know him personally.'

Randi gave a rueful shrug. 'No, I don't, sad to say. I'm afraid he's out of my league.'

Since Randi's latest love interest was a young Superior Court judge, Jane couldn't imagine that even the most eligible and élitist man in Seattle could possibly be out of her league.

'I can't believe that, Randi,' she said. 'You could have any man you wanted.'

Randi flashed her a dazzling smile. 'What a nice woman you are, Jane Fairchild,' she said warmly. 'Not an envious bone in your body, is there? But, then, you've got your nice Robert sewn up tight and aren't really interested in men like Blake Bannister.'

Of course I'm not, Jane said to herself. Then, aloud, she said, 'I still don't understand why you say he's out of your league.'

'He's engaged, that's why. To Monica Mason, no less.'

'I see what you mean,' Jane said.

Monica Mason was as high as Seattle high society reached. She travelled in that rarefied circle of opera and symphony patrons, the exclusive stratum of jet setters and wealthy old families that lived entirely set apart in their waterfront homes that dotted the shores of Lake Washington, with their yachts and their private aeroplanes.

Well, that's that, Jane thought as she went back to her table and resumed work on the layout she'd been puzzling over before the interruption. Not only was he gorgeous, but he was Seattle society. She could still enjoy looking at him, she thought, as she tried different positions for the photographs on top of the worktable.

Jane was nothing if not sensible and realistic. She prided herself on facing facts squarely, on doing what was possible and accepting her limitations. She had learned years ago the folly of making herself miserable over what she couldn't have. She knew, too, that she had a lot to be grateful for.

As she drove across the Lake Washington

floating bridge on her way to her home on Mercer Island that night after work, she dutifully recounted them to herself. At only twenty-six she had a plummy job on *Northwest Life Magazine* that was challenging and used her two best skills of nature photography and gardening. She lived in a comfortable home, left in her care by her parents, who had gone travelling in their retirement, pulling along an expensive and luxurious trailer to points south.

And there was Robert. Why, she wondered, as she parked her little Fiat in the garage, did she find it necessary to remind herself so often about Robert, as though he were some kind of consolation prize? Robert was wonderful, a fine man who cared a lot about her and whom she would probably marry some day.

She pulled the garage door shut and went out into the back garden. It was not quite dark and still warm from the mild sunny afternoon. She liked to inspect her garden every night after work, and took great delight in the lovely little world she had created since her parents left a year ago.

She wandered down the brick path to the rose garden, inspected the crisp reddish new leaves for signs of aphids, and made a mental note to spray for mildew and black spot at the weekend. The yellow forsythia was blazing against the back fence, with clusters of orange, white and golden daffodils blooming underneath. The crocuses were almost finished, the hyacinths just beginning to show colour, and some early Red Emperor tulips made brilliant splashes of scarlet in the front of the rose bed.

She checked the irises for traces of slugs, the bane of every northwest gardener in the damp cool climate, and she clenched her teeth grimly when she saw the faint silvery tracks left on the tender new iris leaves by the slimy disgusting creatures.

'You've had it this time,' she said aloud as she marched into the house to get out the box of pellets.

She stood out in the back for a long time, sprinkling the slug bait around the dahlia bed while she was at it, and thinking about her date with Robert tonight. Although he wasn't a music lover, he was considerate enough to treat her to an occasional concert. Tonight they were going to Meany Hall at the University to hear the Philadelphia String Quartet play a concert of Mozart chamber music. She'd promised him dinner in exchange for the favour, and she should get started on it.

Good old Robert, she thought warmly, as she went into the kitchen and washed her hands at the sink. He was so good to her, so reliable, so dependable. And, a little voice whispered, so dull.

By six o'clock, a rich crab casserole was bubbling in the oven, the greens were all prepared for a tossed salad, and Jane was in the shower. The concert started at eight. They had planned to eat dinner at six-thirty, and Robert was always prompt.

After she dried off, she went into the bedroom to get dressed. With a little thrill of anticipation, she pulled open her lingerie drawer. She smiled to herself with secret satisfaction at the neat piles of sheer, lacy, gorgeous underclothes, much of it handmade and all of it expensive.

It was her one extravagance, a luxury she indulged, a covert passion she shared with no one. It made her feel almost as though she were leading a double life. Her outer appearance was conservative to the point of dullness. That was the image she wanted to project to the world, the public role in which she felt most comfortable. But it did wonders for her confidence and morale as a woman to know that next to her skin was the finest silk, the most delicate lace, the sheerest linen.

What the world would see tonight at the concert was a sensible young woman dressed in a well-tailored navy blue woollen suit, a discreetly polka-dotted long-sleeved blouse with a little tie at the neck, and a pair of medium-heeled cordovan pumps. Her thick shiny hair would be brushed and combed neatly in its usual style, her strong-boned, rather thin face would be free of make-up except for a dash of lipstick, and she would set no man's pulses racing, nor turn one masculine head.

Beneath the bland surface, however, unknown even to Robert, she would be dressed like a *femme fatâle*, the most flamboyant courtesan.

Tonight, she chose a scantily cut, flesh-coloured silk teddy. She giggled a little wickedly as she pulled it on over her bare skin, then viewed herself in the mirror. It was cut extremely low in front so that the deep V revealed the entire upper half of her firm breasts and the cleavage between them. The material was not quite sheer, but the thrust of her nipples was unmistakably visible.

If poor Robert only knew, she thought with a self-satisfied smile as she smoothed her hands over the silky fabric. Why, she wondered idly, was it always 'poor' Robert in her mind? He would be so shocked if he ever saw her like this.

Then suddenly, unbidden, the image of Blake Bannister flashed into her mind, and she wondered what she would find in those piercing blue eyes if he could see her now. Not shock, she was certain.

With a mild feeling of regret, she quickly drew a full slip over her head. It was getting late. Robert would be here any minute now.

There was nothing really wrong with Robert, she thought, as she watched him across from her at the dining-room table. He was actually quite good-looking in a sandy-haired, colourless way. He was extremely polite and very considerate. He never insisted on his own way and wouldn't dream of forcing her into lovemaking. Sometimes she wondered if he was even interested in sex, if perhaps she might not be able to feel desire for him if he only showed a little passion for her.

He was explaining something to her now about his latest anti-trust case, a subject she found extremely boring, but for which she tried valiantly to summon up a spark of enthusiasm.

'So you see,' he said, between bites of the crab casserole, 'the discovery process is really the most critical part of the preparation of the case.'

He gave her an expectant look, as though waiting for confirmation of a statement she didn't begin to comprehend, nor care about. She gazed at him blankly.

'It all sounds very complicated,' she murmured, just to be saying something.

Actually, she thought, as he launched into a long commentary on the intricacies of document inspection, he doesn't really care whether I understand or not. It was enough for him that she listen attentively and make an occasional vague remark to show she cared.

I do care, she thought, warming towards him. Robert was very dear to her. She'd known him all her life, since schooldays. They'd started first grade together. Their families had been friends. They'd never discussed marriage, were not engaged, officially or unofficially, and had just kind of drifted into a comfortable attachment where they took each other's presence for granted.

'What do you hear from your parents?' he was asking her now.

She stood up and started collecting their plates. 'They're having a wonderful time,' she replied. 'They love Florida. I talked to them last weekend, and Dad still feels he did the right thing by taking an early retirement.'

She was standing over him now, reaching in front of him for his wineglass. She stared down at the top of his head and noticed for the first time that the sandy hair was not as thick as it used to be. There was no bald spot, but she could see his scalp at the crown where his parting began.

Suddenly, an idea occurred to her. He was just her age, twenty-six. While they saw each other often, sometimes a week or two would go by when he wouldn't call. His attitude towards her was always affectionate, considerate and warm but, aside from an occasional hug or a tepid good night kiss, she'd never seen the slightest indication of passion in him.

Was it possible that Robert had a sex life she knew nothing about? The idea was so new to her that she paused for a moment with her hand in mid-air on its way to the wineglass, to think it over. If so, she wondered, would it bother her? She decided to find out.

'Robert,' she said slowly. He turned his head to

look up at her. 'Robert, do you see other women? Besides me, I mean.'

His face immediately went up in flame. He opened his mouth, but no sound came out. He just sat there, staring at her, his eyes wide with shocked surprise.

She knew, then. Of course. Well, she thought, while she waited for him to collect himself, how do I feel about it? To her intense surprise, all she felt was a strong surge of relief, and it dawned on her then that much of her attachment to Robert, aside from sheer force of habit, was based on a fear of hurting him.

She smiled at him and put a hand on his shoulder. She could feel the muscles bunch up under her fingers from the tension her question had created in him.

'It's OK, Robert,' she said kindly, 'you don't have to answer that.' She gave his shoulder a little squeeze and moved away from him to finish clearing the table.

She felt his eyes on her as she worked, but she didn't want to embarrass him further by saying anything more or even looking at him. She carried the tray of dishes out into the kitchen, calling to him over her shoulder as she went.

'I think we'd better get going. I'll save the dishes for later.'

She put the dirty dishes in the sink and ran water over them to let them soak. She glanced around the kitchen. A neat cook, she always cleared up after herself as she went. She dried her hands and went back into the dining-room.

Robert was standing at the window, his hands in his pockets, looking out at the gathering dusk. It was raining gently and would be dark soon. Jane

felt a rush of sympathy for him and regretted her
idle question.

'I'll just get my raincoat and umbrella,' she said
as she passed by behind him. 'Then we can leave.'

The concert was wonderful, as always. Meany Hall
was a small auditorium, and perfect for the
intimate chamber music played by the quartet.
Jane loved music, Mozart especially, and was so
enthralled by the concert that she forgot all about
the awkwardness between them at dinner.

On the way home in the dark, they spoke only
of the music, comparing it to that of another
famous string quartet they'd heard last year, until
they were on the floating bridge. It was raining
harder now, and Robert, as always, drove very
carefully over the greasy road surface.

'I've been thinking over your question,' he said
at last. His eyes were fixed firmly on the road
ahead, and he didn't look at her when he spoke.

'What question?' Jane asked. Then she remembered. 'Oh, *that* question.' She turned to him
and put a hand on his arm. 'I'm sorry if I upset
you, Robert. I had no right even to ask it.
Honestly, it doesn't matter. I was just curious.'

Robert manoeuvred the car carefully around the
wide bulge at the eastern end of the bridge, and
now they were on the island. He took the turn off
the highway that led to her house before he spoke
again.

'You took me by surprise, that's all,' he said.
'It's bothered me a little, I guess I've felt a little
guilty about it. I've wanted to tell you, but the
time never seemed right.'

Jane felt a sharp sad pang of regret. She would
miss Robert. Then, she thought, but if he's in love,

I'm glad for him. She wondered if she was jealous. She did feel a touch of jealousy, she realised, but not that he was in love with someone else. She envied the fact that he was in love at all. It was an experience she had missed, and what she resented was the fact that he was able to feel an emotion that apparently was denied her.

He parked in front of her house, shut off the ignition, and turned to her.

'I'm not very proud of what I've done,' he said in a miserable tone of voice. 'She was just available, that's all.' He hesitated. 'You know all those trips I've had to take to Los Angeles in the past year for document inspection?' he went on.

'Robert,' she interrupted, 'honestly you don't have to explain anything to me. We're just old friends, after all. I'm happy for you. Is it serious?'

He turned on her, then, his eyes staring in disbelief. 'Lord, no, it's not serious! It was just— well—physical. As I said, she was available. I just kind of fell into it. But you've got to believe me, Jane, it means nothing to me. Nothing at all.'

'I don't understand, Robert.' She was confused now, even a little angry. While the thought of losing Robert's companionship had given her a definite pang, the belief that he had fallen in love with someone brought her only relief, as though she could now set down a burden she had been carrying all her life.

'Actually,' he went on in a solemn tone, 'I think that while I'm a little ashamed of what I've done, good has come of it. It made me realise how much I care for you. Whenever I was with—her—I couldn't help comparing her to you, wishing it was you.'

'Robert,' she whispered, appalled. 'What are you saying?'

He reached out to put his arms around her and pulled her up against him awkwardly. 'I'm saying I love you, Jane. You're what I want. We've been good friends all our lives, now I want it to be something more. I think we should get married.'

He kissed her roughly, then, on the mouth. Jane was so stunned by his declaration of love, so totally unprepared for his proposal, that she just sat passively in his arms and tried to collect her thoughts. As his mouth moved on hers, it dawned on her that the sensation did absolutely nothing to her. Her heartbeat continued on its slow, steady pace. Instead of a wild surge of desire, she experienced only a mild annoyance, and when she felt his tongue press against her tightly closed lips, she pulled away from him.

'Robert,' she said calmly, 'you've taken me completely by surprise.'

Gently, she disengaged herself from his embrace. He was panting shallowly through his mouth and obviously aroused. This astonished her. She didn't want to hurt him, but neither could she manufacture feelings just to suit him.

He was grinning at her now. 'I know. I understand. It surprised me, too, when I finally realised how I felt. I won't rush you, but I think when you get used to the idea, you'll find it's a pretty good one.'

Jane shook her head. 'I don't know,' she said cautiously. 'I don't know if I *can* think of you that way.'

'Just promise me you'll consider it.'

'All right. I can do that.'

*   *   *

Lying in bed that night, Jane did think it over—
and over. But she always came to the same
conclusion. She didn't love Robert, not in the way
he seemed to love her. The thought of physical
passion with him simply left her cold. But why?
She did love him, but as a good friend, not as a
lover.

I must be frigid, she decided at last. She
thought back over the dates she'd had in the
past. It seemed as though she'd spent all her
time fending off groping hands, wet thrusting
tongues and aroused male bodies pressed up
against her.

Was physical desire an experience forever barred
to her? If so, then she might as well marry Robert.
He loved her. He'd make a wonderful husband
and father. They'd build a good life together. Her
parents and his would be ecstatic.

She'd give it serious consideration, at least, she
finally decided. It was definitely worth that.
Probably lots of women never felt passion, but
that didn't mean they couldn't be good wives and
mothers.

Satisfied at last, she rolled over and began to
drift off to sleep. As she let go, however, she
became aware of a little nagging thought that
tugged at her unconscious mind demanding
attention. She couldn't quite make it out. It was an
image of some kind, and she knew it had to do
with her lingering doubts about entering into a
marriage without passion, but she couldn't quite
put her finger on it.

Just as she went over the edge into sleep, she
caught a fleeting glimpse of it. The image clarified
in her mind, and her whole body became suffused
with warmth at the vision of a stern, dark-haired

man with piercing blue eyes. It was her last conscious thought.

Robert called her at work the next day to tell her he had to go out of town for depositions on his anti-trust case and didn't know how long he'd be gone. Jane was relieved. He wouldn't be pressing her for an answer to his proposal for a while. She still hadn't definitely made up her mind.

'Where are you going?' she asked idly. The models were at the window again, and Jane watched them as she spoke to Robert. Today they were holding up messages for the benefit of the workmen.

'I'm going to Los Angeles,' Robert replied, 'but you don't need to worry. I'm not going to see her again.'

'Oh, Robert,' she said abruptly, 'it's all right.' She was annoyed at herself for even asking. 'I don't care.'

He chuckled. 'That's just like you, Jane, to be so big about it, so understanding. But I promise, it's over.'

When she hung up the phone, she was still frowning in exasperation at Robert's refusal to believe she really meant it when she said she didn't care what he did. She met Randi's curious gaze from across the room. She got up and walked over to her, wondering if she should confide her reservations about Robert's proposal to the tall blonde.

'Trouble?' Randi asked. 'You look as though our beloved editor has just blackballed your latest full-colour posy spread.'

Jane shook her head and smiled. 'No, it's not that. It's Robert.'

Randi raised one perfect eyebrow. 'Ah, trouble in paradise?'

'Paradise? What on earth are you talking about?'

Randi shrugged. 'You've got it made, kid. You're the envy of us all. You never get involved with unsuitable men. You never get your heart broken. You're sensible, cool, unflappable. And you've got a paragon of an up-and-coming young lawyer at your feet.'

Jane was astonished. 'Is that what people think?'

'Of course.' Randi gestured towards the window, where Stephanie and Jennifer were giggling and holding up their messages. 'I don't see you making a fool of yourself over those hunks across the way.'

Jane looked out of the window then. Two brawny workmen were holding up a large white placard with a big red heart painted in the centre. One of them put a hand over his own heart and imitated a swooning posture, while the other doubled up in a fit of laughter.

Then, in the background, she saw Blake Bannister striding forward, his arms crossed over his chest. He had on worn jeans, a sleeveless down jacket over a plaid shirt, heavy boots and a hard hat. He came to the very edge of the floor where the two clowns were standing and tapped one of them on the shoulder.

Immediately, the placard fell to the ground and the two men scurried away. The tall man stood there alone for a moment, his legs apart, his knuckles resting on his slim hips, frowning after the men. Jane couldn't take her eyes off him. She stared as he slowly reached up, took off the hard hat and ran his hand over the shock of thick dark hair. He couldn't have been more than twenty feet away, and once again she recognised the strong features and flashing blue eyes of the man she had run into the night of Fat Tuesday.

Suddenly, he looked up. His stern gaze swept over the giggling models, and slowly a wide grin began to spread on his face. He shrugged helplessly, and saluted them briefly with the hard hat before clapping it back on his head. Then he turned and strode away, his hands tucked behind him in the back pockets of his jeans.

'That is one gorgeous man,' Randi murmured beside her.

Jane's knees felt weak. 'Yes,' she agreed.

Randi turned to her. 'That's what I mean when I say you're lucky to have Robert. He'll never break your heart, like that one would.' She sighed deeply. 'But what I'd give to get a chance at him!' she breathed fervently.

As it turned out, Robert was gone for over a month. He went from Los Angeles to Tuscon to Santa Fe on the trail of his witnesses, and didn't feel it was worthwhile to fly all the way back to Seattle just for a few days at the weekends.

'Besides,' he said over the telephone one night in late April when he called her from Santa Fe, 'it's probably better for us to be separated for a while. Give you time to think.'

She couldn't have agreed more. As the days passed, she was coming more and more to believe that the safe, sane, practical, sensible, prudent thing to do was to marry Robert and get it over with. But was that the right kind of attitude with which to enter into a lifetime commitment?

The garden occupied most of her evenings and

weekends these days. She loved the profuse florescence of spring. Every day brought a new splash of colour into her carefully planned garden. With the fading of the forsythia and flowering crab-apple came the tall brilliant tulips, the flowering quince, the early cherry blossoms.

Work on the building next door seemed to be progressing at a virtual snail's pace. In early May the carpenters went on strike, and there was a week's blessed silence in the office as all pounding ceased. Stephanie and Jennifer grumbled over the disappearance of their entertainment, but at least the May issue of *Northwest Life Magazine* came out on time. By the following Monday, the men were back on the job, and the models were once again at the window.

Jane had to admit she wasn't sorry to see them again herself, even though it meant having to get used to the noise again. She'd missed her daily glimpses of Blake Bannister. His presence across the way was like a little treat she gave herself, a secret pleasure she'd come to look forward to. She enjoyed just looking at him and, although she didn't hang at the window as the others did, she managed to make sure she had a good look at his tall form at least once a day.

On Wednesday of that week, much to her dismay, she woke up with a badly swollen jaw and a toothache that seemed to fill her whole mouth with a searing pain. It felt as though the top of her head would come off at any minute. On her last visit to the dentist to have her teeth cleaned, he'd made ominous noises about a wisdom tooth that looked impacted, warning her that, if it started giving her trouble, it would have to come out.

When she got to the office, the constant din

from the building under construction only made it worse. Each whine of the saw and bang of the hammer sent her throbbing jaw into a paroxysm of sheer agony. She was sitting at her desk with her head in her hands trying to concentrate on the June garden layout, when Randi came over to her and stood looking down at her.

'You really better do something about that tooth, Jane,' she said. 'You look like a squirrel with a nut in its cheek.'

Jane glared up at her with miserable eyes. 'Thanks a lot. You're making me feel much better.'

Randi smiled. 'Come on, you're not the martyr type! You're our sensible Jane who always does the right thing.'

Jane lowered her eyes guiltily. 'I hate the dentist,' she muttered.

'Who doesn't? Now, call him.'

Jane made a face at her, then sighed and reached for the phone. When she explained the situation to Mr Richardson, he told her he could fit her in at two o'clock that afternoon.

Somehow, with the help of aspirin and sheer force of will, Jane made it through until one-thirty. By that time she was in such pain that her usual fear and trembling at the prospect of spending time in Mr Richardson's torture chamber was forgotten. All she wanted was to get rid of that awful throbbing. It seemed to her by now that she must have been born with it.

As she gathered her things and walked towards the door, Randi glanced up from her desk and gave her a sympathetic look.

'Will you be OK?' she asked. 'Do you want me to go with you?'

Jane managed a lop-sided smile. 'No, thanks. I'll
be all right. It's only a tooth, after all, not major
surgery.'

Jennifer called to her from the window. 'Don't
be too sure,' she said encouragingly. 'My sister
had to have ten stiches in her jaw and was flat on
her back for a week after . . .'

'Oh, Jennifer, shut up!' Randi snapped. She
turned back to Jane. 'How will you get home?'

'I'll take the bus. I knew something like this was
going to happen when I woke up like this this
morning,' she pointed to her tender jaw, 'so I
didn't drive in. I'll be all right once the tooth is
out.'

Randi didn't look convinced. 'Well, OK, but if
you need a ride home, give me a call and I'll come
and get you.'

'Thanks, Randi.' She squared her shoulders in a
parody of going bravely into battle, and marched
out of the door.

CHAPTER THREE

IT was a beautiful day, warm and sunny, but as Jane trudged miserably through the crowds on the five blocks to the Medical-Dental Building, she didn't even notice the begonias and *impatiens* blooming in the small bed in front of the building or the flowering cherries that lined Fourth Avenue. All she could think of was getting rid of that awful pain in her jaw.

The extraction procedure, however, turned out to be far more complicated and unnerving than she had anticipated. Blessed with strong healthy teeth, with only a few minor fillings, she was totally unprepared for the enormous needle that pumped the novocaine into her jaw, or the grinding crunching noise Mr Richardson's instruments of torture made while he dug for the elusive wisdom tooth. All that blood unsettled her, too, and he did indeed take several stitches.

By the time it was over, she felt as though she'd just had half her head cut off or been in a terrible accident. She was utterly limp, weak and perspiring, and she stumbled out of the dentist's chair like a zombie.

'Is someone driving you home?' Mr Richardson asked.

She thought about Randi, but when she called the office, there was no answer. 'If I could just sit down for a while,' she said weakly, 'maybe I can try again in a few minutes.'

Out in the waiting-room she sat down, laid her

head back on the chair and closed her eyes. At least, she told herself, the pain was gone and she was out of that awful chair.

Her relief was so great that in a few minutes she began to feel almost euphoric. Little by little, her strength returned. There's no need to bother Randi, she thought. All I need is some fresh air. She decided that the sensible thing to do was to walk back to the office. Her bus stopped right in front of the building. If she felt too weak to get home on her own, she'd take Randi up on her offer of a lift.

She stopped off at the rest-room to splash a little cold water on her face and comb her hair. There, that's not so bad, she said to herself as she peered into the mirror. The swelling was gone, and apart from a numb lip and a slightly dazed look in her eyes, she was fine.

She took the lift down and went out on to the pavement. For some reason, the jostling crowds unsettled her. I'm just a little weak, she thought, all I have to do is walk five blocks, and she started to move a little faster.

With each block, however, her step faltered a little more. The novocaine was beginning to wear off, and she was becoming gradually aware of an ominous, unpleasant, tingling sensation in her jaw. Mr Richardson had given her some Codeine tablets, but she didn't dare take one until she was safely inside her own house.

By the time she arrived back at the Cascade Building, dragging her feet every step of the last block, she had begun to worry quite seriously about her condition. Her head was spinning, her knees felt weak, and the tingling in her jaw had become raw pain. She wasn't even sure now she could make it into the building and up the lift to find Randi.

A wave of blackness passed over her, and she began to panic. What am I going to do? she thought, as she reached out blindly to find something to hang on to. The wooden bus shelter was just ahead. If she could just make it a few more steps, she'd be all right. At the first step, however, she felt her knees buckle, felt herself falling, then came up against something hard, and dimly she resigned herself to fainting on the street.

Instead, something held her up. She didn't fall. A firm support was gripping her arms. Her eyes fluttered open and she looked up dizzily into a familiar bright blue gaze.

'Oh, no,' she groaned, 'not again,' and lost consciousness.

The next thing she knew, she was in a car driving across Lake Washington. She opened her eyes and blinked at the sudden glare of bright sunlight that was reflected on the water. Gingerly, she moved her head to the right. The majestic white peak of Mount Rainier looked up in the south in solitary splendour.

She turned her eyes to the left, then, and focused them groggily on the strong profile of Blake Bannister. She couldn't quite grasp what had happened yet. Was she still unconscious? Dreaming? She blinked and tried to clear her head, but when she opened her eyes again, he was still there.

She studied him for a moment, trying to assimilate the strange disorientating situation. He was dressed in his work clothes, a red and black plaid shirt open at the neck to reveal his tanned throat. She glanced at his hands on the steering wheel, large hands, workman's hands, strong and well-formed, with a trace of grime on them from his day on the job.

It was his profile, though, that held her gaze. A strong chin, wide bony jaw, finely-sculptured mouth, straight nose, he was just as she remembered him from the night of Fat Tuesday. And then there were the eyes, half-closed now as he squinted a little in the glare off the lake, but still revealing a line of that vivid blue.

Suddenly, he glanced over at her. Still groggy, she wasn't quick enough to look away, and she found herself held captive by that blue gaze. He smiled at her, then, and her heart gave a strong flip-flop.

'Well, Jane,' he said, 'we meet again.'

Oh, Lord, she thought, he remembered. She jerked herself upright and immediately closed her eyes with a groan as the pain shot through her jaw. She felt horribly embarrassed. What must he think of her? They'd met twice, and both times she was on the verge of passing out. Why, she thought in frustration, did he have to remember? All her life she had been the girl everyone forgot, so that she was long accustomed to thinking of herself as decidedly unmemorable. Now, when someone did remember, it had to be because she'd made a fool of herself. Twice.

'How do you know my name?' she asked weakly.

'Simple. When you passed out on me again, I looked in your bag, found your driver's licence. You know. Name and address?'

She thought this over. 'That took a lot of nerve,' she said sternly.

He raised his eyebrows at that. 'Oh? Would you rather I'd left you on the pavement? Or maybe I should have called an ambulance and created a real sensation.' He gave her hard look. 'You're an ungrateful little thing, aren't you?'

She looked down at her lap where her hands were tightly clutching her bag. 'I'm sorry,' she mumbled, 'I'm not quite myself.'

'Are you drunk again?' he asked pleasantly. 'You know, you really should do something about that bad habit of yours.'

'No, I'm not drunk!' she cried. 'I just had an impacted wisdom tooth pulled, and it hit me harder than I thought it would.'

He nodded. 'I figured it was something like that.' He gave her a sidelong glance. 'You don't look like the type to wander around the streets in the middle of the day half-sloshed.'

'I should hope not,' she said primly.

They were off the bridge now and heading past the Mercer Island business district towards her street.

'Now that you know I'm your rescuer,' he said, 'aren't you ashamed of yourself for snapping at me?'

'I've already apologised for that,' she said. 'It was just a shock to be downtown on Fourth Avenue one minute and in a car with a strange man the next.'

They were on her street now, and he was peering at the numbers on the letter boxes. She pointed out her house to him, and he pulled up at the kerb.

He turned to her. 'I'm not a strange man,' he said as he pulled on the brake and switched off the engine. 'We've been neighbours for quite a while now.'

With that, he got out of the car, and she watched as he crossed in front then came round to open her door. He leaned down and reached inside for her.

'What are you doing?' she asked as one arm went under her knees and the other came round her waist.

'I'm carrying you,' he explained patiently. He pulled her out of the car and held her up, then kicked the door shut and started walking up the path. 'Nice garden,' he said, looking around as he went.

He had moved too fast for her to protest. I might as well relax and enjoy it, she thought. She leaned against him and allowed him to carry her. Next door, her neighbour, Mrs Hall, was gazing at the spectacle with undisguised interest as she watered her flower-bed. If her jaw hadn't hurt so much, Jane thought, it would have been funny. She almost waved at her.

It was only a short walk from the kerb to the front door but, in that time, Jane was aware of some strange sensations warring within her. On the one hand she was a little embarrassed at the situation, but on the other, it was very pleasant to be carried, apparently with no visible effort, by this tall, strong, and, yes, gorgeous man.

'Key?' he said at the door.

She reached into her handbag and pulled out her key-ring. He set her down gently and carefully, one arm still holding her close, while he unlocked the door. As she leaned against him, the rough fabric of his shirt scratching her cheek, the thought crossed her mind that what she was experiencing, for the first time in her life, was a powerful physical attraction.

She was intensely, almost painfully, aware of his sheer masculinity. Everything about him was so pre-eminently *male*! She could see the dark bristles on his jaw, feel the hard muscles of his arms, his chest, smell the faintly musky odour of a man who had been hard at work all day. She thought about Robert. He and Blake Bannister could have belonged to different species, the contrast between them was so pronounced.

Then she felt him leading her inside, and she began to come to her senses. Not only was this man a virtual stranger, but he was a noted member of what passed for high society in Seattle. If he was out of the lovely Randi's league, she certainly had no business thinking of him in any way that was remotely personal.

Inside the house, he led her to a chair in the living-room, and she sank down gratefully into its familiar contours. She laid her head back and closed her eyes, the pain in her jaw so excruciating now that she could blot out all her disturbing thoughts of Blake Bannister without much effort.

He was leaning over her now, his hands braced on the arms of the chair.

'Do you have anything for the pain?' he asked softly.

She pointed to her handbag. He opened it and took out the packet of capsules Mr Richardson had given her. He left her then, and in a few moments he was back with a glass of water. He sat down on the arm of the chair and put a hand on the back of her head, supporting it while she swallowed the Codeine.

'I think you'd better lie down,' he said. 'That's potent stuff if you're not used to it.'

She nodded weakly, then felt him pick her up

again and carry her down the hall to her bedroom.
He laid her on the bed and pulled her shoes off. As
she slipped into unconsciousness, she was dimly
aware of being covered with a blanket, a cool hand
on her forehead, and then oblivion.

When she awoke, it was growing dark outside. The
inside of her mouth felt dry and sticky and filled
with the most loathsome taste she'd ever known,
but the pain was gone at last. There was only a
dull ache there now to remind her of the
afternoon's ordeal.

She felt so much better after her rest that she
could even smile at the way Blake Bannister had
rescued her for the second time. He was a very nice
man, she thought, and she'd always be grateful to
him. She'd probably never see him again, she
realised, except across the way in the office. Even
then, as soon as the floor they were working on
was finished, she wouldn't even have that pleasure.

What she wanted right now was a shower, a
careful tooth-brushing and then something to eat.
A bowl of soup, maybe, or an omelette. Mr
Richardson had warned her to be careful, with
dire threats of dry sockets if she disturbed the
wound.

She had just sat up and was swinging her legs
over the side of the bed when she heard strange
noises coming from another part of the house. It
sounded like the rattle of dishes, then footsteps, and
before she had time to be alarmed, a grinning
Blake Bannister appeared at her bedroom door.

'Well, sleeping beauty, how do you feel?'

The sight of him leaning in the doorway, his
broad shoulders almost filling it, his jeans-clad
long legs crossed casually, almost took her breath

away. She had her strength back now, however, and with it her self-possession. She had learned long ago not to allow herself to long for something she knew she couldn't have, and she wasn't going to start now.

'What are you doing here?' she asked. She stood up and smoothed down her wrinkled skirt.

'I'm tending the sick,' he said in a hurt tone. 'Are you hungry? By the way, I'm quite harmless. My name is Blake Bannister, and, as I say, we've been virtually neighbours during the construction downtown.'

She looked at him, genuinely surprised that he had recognised her in the office. She hadn't spent that much time at the window. It occurred to her then that this man was far from harmless, as he claimed. What could he want from her?

'How does a bowl of soup sound?' he asked. 'I found a few cans in the cupboard and heated some up.'

'I'm glad to see you make yourself right at home,' she said a little drily.

'Now, now, don't get testy. I told you I'm harmless.'

He didn't, however, look in the least harmless to Jane. He was the kind of man who filled a room with his presence, not only because he was large, but through the sheer force of his commanding attitude. He had simply taken charge of her life in the same way he took charge of his men on the job, and she wasn't at all sure she liked it.

'I guess I could eat something,' she said at last.

As she followed him down the hallway to the kitchen, she thought to herself that she would give him the benefit of the doubt and assume he was only being a good Samaritan. After dinner, he would leave, and that would be the end of it. It would be utter folly to imagine that a man like Blake Bannister would ever be attracted to plain Jane.

The kitchen was the focal point of the house, a long narrow room that stretched across the whole back width and offered a view of the garden Jane tended so lovingly. Half the room was actually a dining area, separated from the work space by an island counter and comfortably furnished with a round birch table, captain's chairs, and a large open china-cupboard on one wall. There were bright chintz cushions on the chairs, a braided rug on the floor and floral watercolours Jane had painted herself on the walls. The whole back wall was glass, with sliding doors leading out on to a small brick patio.

'I really like your garden,' Blake said as he ladled out soup into bowls. 'Who planned it for you?'

'Well, I guess I did,' she said. 'This is really my parents' house, you see, and neither one of them was ever interested in gardening. The whole back was covered with grass and a few shrubs for years. Then, when I started getting interested in growing things, they just turned it over to me, and it's been my garden ever since.'

He set their bowls of soup on the table and sat down across from her. She noticed that he had also fixed himself a very large sandwich with what looked like every kind of cold meat she had on hand, plus cheese, lettuce and tomatoes.

'So, you live here with your parents, then?' he asked.

She watched, entranced, as he took a healthy bite of sandwich and began to chew. There was something about the way the fine bony jaw worked, and his whole bearing of supreme, casual self-assurance, that fascinated her.

'No,' she replied at last. She stirred the hot soup around in the bowl. 'They're living in Florida at the moment in a mobile home. Dad retired early last year from Boeing—he's an aeronautical engineer—and they decided to travel.'

'You live here alone then? No brothers or sisters?'

She eyes him warily. He was drinking a glass of milk now, his head tipped back, and as she watched his long throat working, she almost laughed aloud at her suspicions. A man who looked like he did would never pose a threat to her virtue.

'Yes, I live alone,' she said calmly. She took a spoonful of soup, careful to keep it away from the right side of her mouth where the tooth had been extracted.

'Tell me,' he said, 'what you and your three beautiful companions do in that office across the way.' He shook his head and laughed. 'I'm not sure we'll ever get off that floor unless I put blinkers on my men.'

Jane was stung in spite of herself at the allusion to her 'three beautiful companions'. The obvious interpretation was that they were definitely in a different category from her. She'd thought she'd become used to that, and it bothered her that this man had the power to open the old wound.

'We all work on *Northwest Life Magazine*,' she explained, 'but in different departments. We only share a room. One of them, Randi Tatum, the blonde, is the fashion editor, and the other two are her models.'

'Ah,' he said with a lift of heavy dark eyebrows. 'I thought they looked familiar. And what's your job?'

'I'm the garden editor,' she said stiffly.

She was suddenly very angry at herself. She'd made the job she'd worked so hard to get and had taken such pride in doing well sound like the booby prize in a beauty contest.

He nodded. 'That explains the garden,' he said.

He pushed his chair back and stood up abruptly, glancing at his watch. Jane continued to eat her soup while he cleared the table and rinsed out his dishes at the sink. She knew he would be leaving, and was surprised at how bereft this made her feel.

When she finished her soup, she got up and carried her bowl to the sink. He took it from her wordlessly and they stood there together while he rinsed it out and set it down with the others. They were only inches apart. Jane was reminded of how he'd carried her into the house earlier, and the sensations she'd felt then returned now as she watched him out of the corner of her eye.

The potency of his presence went far beyond his good looks. It was in his whole bearing; the casual way he stood at the sink, legs slightly apart, shoulders bent over. The grace of his movements as he handled the dishes. The expression on his fine features, so intent on what he was doing, yet relaxed. Whatever it was, she thought, if he bottled it, he'd be a millionaire.

'There,' he said, reaching for a bunch of paper towels to dry his hands. He turned to her. 'Sure you'll be OK?'

'Oh, yes,' she said with a smile. 'Thank you for everything.'

She walked with him to the door, suddenly anxious for him to leave. She felt somewhat as she might if she'd been on a shopping expedition and seen a beautiful fur coat which she knew she couldn't afford. It was better in the long run to pass on, to refuse to even contemplate having it for herself. The longer he stayed, she was positive, the harder it would be when he left.

'Thank you again,' she said at the door. 'I'm sorry to have taken you out of your way.'

'Oh, I live in Fall City,' he said. 'Mercer Island is right on my way home.'

'I see. Goodbye, then.'

'See you later,' he said, and turned to go.

She wanted very much to stand and watch him walk down the path to his car, just for the sheer pleasure of it, but she knew that such pleasures were dangerous in her position. If she gave in to an innocent temptation like that, the next one would be even harder to resist.

She went inside the house and closed the door firmly behind her. The moment she did, the house seemed suddenly empty, and her conviction that she had to put all thoughts of Blake Bannister out of her mind was only confirmed.

Her jaw was throbbing again anyway. Funny how she didn't even notice it when he was here, she thought drily. She went into the kitchen to put the dishes they had used into the dishwasher. Looking down at the plate, the glass, the bowl, the spoon he had used, she was tempted for a moment to leave them there as a reminder that he actually had been there, sitting across from her, standing next to her.

'No, my girl,' she said aloud, 'that won't do.'

She put them in the dishwasher then, and went

down the hall to her room. Her tooth was really hurting now. She took a quick shower, swallowed another Codeine tablet and got into bed.

The next morning she awoke to an overcast sky and the sound of rain pattering against her bedroom window. Her jaw was still aching, and when she saw on the bedside clock that it was past nine anyway, she decided not to go into the office.

After breakfast, she took another Codeine, crawled back into bed and slept the morning away. The insistent ringing of the telephone woke her up around noon. She sat up in bed and reached for it.

'Hello.'

'Jane, it's Robert. How are you? I called the office and they said you were off sick.'

'When did you get back?' she asked, settling her head back on the pillows.

'Late last night. We decided we'd all been away from home too long and are taking a recess for a week or two.'

'That's good,' she said. 'I'm glad you're back. I've missed you.' That wasn't precisely true, she thought; actually, she hadn't given Robert a thought in the month he'd been gone except to ponder how she was going to tell him she didn't want to be engaged.

'I've missed you, too, Jane. Now, how are you and what can I do for you?'

She told him about her wisdom tooth, and assured him she didn't need anything. Actually, the pain had diminished considerably since her morning's nap, and she felt quite like herself again.

'It's really nothing, Robert,' she said. 'I'm not sick. It was nasty, but it seems to be healing nicely.

I plan to go to work tomorrow.'

'Well, I'll drive out to see you tonight, at any rate.'

Although his parents still lived a few blocks away, Robert had moved into his own apartment in the city as soon as he'd finished law school three years ago and started his first job.

'Fine,' she said, 'around seven. I can fix us an omelette or something.'

'Jane,' he said. She waited. 'Uh,' he went on hesitantly, 'have you been thinking over what we talked about last month? You know, getting married.'

Married! Somehow that sounded far more serious than getting engaged, and she hadn't even been able to face that.

'I've thought about it,' she said, 'but I haven't really come up with anything definite. It seems like an awfully big step to take.' She hesitated. 'Unless you're quite sure,' she added limply.

'Well, we'll talk about it tonight. See you around seven.'

After they hung up, she got dressed in her old jeans and a cotton shirt. The sun had begun to poke through the clouds, and patches of blue appeared in the leaden sky. She had another bowl of soup for lunch, then went outside to work in the garden. After rain was the best time to look for the slugs that ate virtually everything in sight if you didn't stay on top of them.

One thing led to another, and by the time the sun had moved low in the western sky, Jane was happily shovelling dried manure on to the peonies. During the afternoon, as she worked, she found her thoughts straying to Blake Bannister, and every time they did so, her heart would flop over uncomfortably. Each time this happened, she managed firmly to direct her thoughts elsewhere.

She was just digging in the last sack of manure when she heard the front doorbell ring. She wiped her forehead with the back of her arm and glanced at her watch. She was appalled to see that it was almost six o'clock.

She scraped off her feet on the back doormat and ran through the house to the front door, wondering if Robert had decided to come early. It didn't matter. He'd seen her in worse condition than she was in now, reeking of manure, in her oldest, filthiest clothes and with a dirt-encrusted trowel still in her gloved hand.

When she opened the door, then, to a grinning Blake Bannister, she could only stand there, paralysed, goggling up at him. He was wearing work clothes again and carrying a load of white paper bags. He held them up.

'Chinese food,' he said. 'I figured that's one thing you could manage with your wounded mouth.'

'Blake,' she finally managed to stammer out. 'What are you doing here?'

'Well, you weren't at work today, so I decided you still needed some of my expert nursing care. Can I come in? We should eat this while it's hot.'

He brushed past her into the house, leaving in his wake the tempting aroma of chow mein. Jane's stomach growled, and she realised she was starving, with only a bowl of soup for lunch. She closed the door. Blake was already in the kitchen. She could hear him humming off-key and the sound of dishes and silverware.

She simply didn't know what to think. The only thing that was crystal clear to her, unmistakable in its visceral and sensual impact, was how really delighted she was to see him, especially after she'd made up her mind she never would again.

She started walking slowly towards the kitchen and, with an effort, summoned up all her common sense, her prudence, her powers of good judgment. What was it he wanted from her? She knew very well it was not her body he lusted after. Not only was it inconceivable that a dashing, successful, highly self-confident man like Blake could possibly view plain, sensible Jane Fairchild as a sex object, but, even with her limited experience of men, she could tell by his casual manner with her, his open friendliness, that he wasn't remotely interested in her in that way.

This didn't disturb her; she didn't expect it. What bothered her was the force of her own attraction for him. He was, quite simply, everything a man should be. Devastatingly good-looking, a pleasure just to watch, he was also kind and considerate. Yesterday he'd been genuinely concerned over her distress.

Finally, just as she came to the kitchen door and caught sight of him making himself utterly at home, she decided it really didn't matter what he wanted because she had absolutely nothing to give him. He looked so wonderful standing there in her kitchen that she decided to just relax and enjoy it while it lasted.

'I came early,' he said as he opened cartons and got out serving spoons, 'so you could give me a tour of the garden after dinner while it was still light.' He looked at her. 'Come on, sit down.'

'Thank you very much,' she murmured.

Ignoring the sarcasm in her tone, he started piling his plate high with sweet and sour spare ribs, fried rice, egg roll and almond chicken. She sat down, served herself a portion, and started to eat.

'Why the garden?' she asked between bites. 'Somehow you don't look to me like the domestic type.'

He paused with his fork in mid-air and gave her a searching look. 'Really? That's very interesting. What type am I, then?'

She flushed slightly, then thought the question over for a moment. 'Well,' she said, 'I see you more in a high-rise condo on the shores of Puget Sound with a berth for your luxurious sailboat. That's when you're not going to charity balls and opening nights at the opera or flying off to Acapulco.'

He threw back his head and laughed for a full minute, his chair tipped back on its rear legs, his feet braced on the floor. Then he leaned forward and pointed his fork at her across the table.

'You're wrong on every single count,' he said triumphantly. 'I'm not at all fond of boats, I detest opera, and I don't have time for charity balls. And while I admit I have been to Acapulco a few times, I doubt if I'll ever go back. Too touristy. Also, I live in a house on six acres of ground up near Snoqualmie Falls.' He shook his head. 'For an intelligent, perceptive woman, you sure struck out that time.'

Intelligent? Perceptive? She didn't know what to say. 'Well,' she finally managed, 'we can't all be right all the time.'

'Actually,' he said, 'that's what I wanted to talk to you about, why I wanted to get a better look at your garden.'

She gazed blankly at him. 'I don't understand.'

He waved a hand impatiently in the air. 'The garden. I like what you've done with it. I've built this house up in the woods, and I need to put in a garden. I want you to plan it for me. I want to hire you.'

CHAPTER FOUR

SHE stared at him. 'Hire me?'

So that's what he wanted from her! It was the last thing she had expected and, after the initial shock of his calm statement had worn off, she realised how disappointed she felt, even deflated. But she wasn't going to let him know that. Now that it was clear to her where matters stood between them, she was on firmer ground, and some of her old confidence returned. He had taken her off-balance and disturbed her equilibrium when he'd barged into her life only yesterday. She hadn't known what to expect then. Now she did.

She pushed a stray lock of hair back from her forehead and gazed at him. He was still as appealing as ever, she thought, but now that the parameters of their relationship were established at last, she found her good sense coming to her rescue, and she could view him now not as a flesh and blood man but somewhat as she might a famous film star who wanted to hire her for a job.

'Well?' he said at last. 'Will you do it?'

She leaned back in her chair and smiled at him pleasantly. 'I couldn't possibly even consider such a thing.'

The dark eyebrows shot up. 'Why on earth not?'

She saw that she'd caught him off guard, ruffled his composure, and she felt an intense surge of satisfaction. He was obviously not used to being turned down by women for any reason. It would do him good.

'I have a job,' she explained patiently.

'Oh, that,' he said, dismissing her job with a wave of his large hand.

'Yes, that!' she exclaimed. She was growing angry. 'It's a darned good job. It may not sound like much to you, but I've worked hard . . .'

'Hey, hold on,' he said, 'I'm sorry. I didn't mean to ruffle your feathers. I only meant that, in your lofty position as garden editor, you surely can pretty much work your own hours, so long as you get your spread in on time.'

He was right, but she wasn't going to admit it. 'That's beside the point. No matter what my hours are, they *are* hours. I probably spend more time on my job than if I were tied to a rigid routine.'

'I said I'd pay you,' he said in a hurt tone. 'I like your work. You can name your own hours, even your own figure.'

For a moment, she was tempted to pull an outrageous amount out of the air, just to see if he'd back down, but in the end she knew she couldn't do it. She was in control of her emotions again, and being near this man in any capacity, even as the paid help, could only mean danger to her.

'No,' she said firmly. 'I'm sorry, but it's not possible.'

He cocked his head to one side. 'Stubborn little thing, aren't you?'

If he meant it as an accusation, she thought, it was wasted on her. She stood up and looked down at him with what she hoped was a look of cool dismissal, but when the blue eyes bored into her with reproach, the erratic thudding in the vicinity of her midriff started up again, and she almost wavered.

At that moment, the front doorbell rang. Startled, she tore her eyes away from his.

'Robert!' she said. She'd forgotten all about him.

'Robert?' Blake asked. 'Who's Robert?'

'He's—he's my fiancé,' she blurted out.

It was the first thing that came into her head. Why had she said such a thing? She sensed dimly that it was partly to show him that at least one man desired her enough to want to marry her, but it also closed the door firmly, irrevocably, on any possibility of emotional entanglement with Blake.

'You're engaged?' he asked.

'Does that surprise you?' she shot back at him, stung.

'Not in the least.' He glanced at her bare ring finger. 'I just hadn't seen any evidence.'

'Well, it's not official yet,' she said stiffly.

'I see.'

The doorbell rang again, and she went to answer it. By the time she was half-way there, Robert was inside the front hall and just shutting the door behind him.

'Hi,' he said. 'Sorry for barging in like this, but I got a little worried when you didn't answer.' He came towards her. 'How are you? You look OK.'

'I'm fine, Robert,' she said a little impatiently.

What a situation, she thought, with Robert here and Blake sitting in the kitchen as though he owned the place. He was probably doing the dishes by now. But when she turned round to go back into the kitchen, there he was, leaning up against the doorway, filling it with his large frame and gazing speculatively at Robert.

'Hi,' he said, strolling casually towards them. He held out a hand to a bewildered Robert. 'I'm

Blake Bannister. You must be Robert. Do you like Chinese food? There's plenty left.'

Robert shot Jane a brief accusing look, then reluctantly shook hands with Blake. It would be funny, Jane thought, if it wasn't so awkward. The look on Robert's face was really comical. And what had got into Blake to assume that proprietary air?

She couldn't help comparing the two men, even though she knew it was unfair to Robert. It was like comparing a great screen idol with the boy next door. For one thing, seeing them together, she realised that Blake was quite a bit older than Robert, probably by eight or nine years. Robert's face seemed somehow unformed, even callow, next to the more pronounced features and more vivid colouring of the older man. There was also a contained look of experience about Blake in the faint lines around his eyes, the set of the firm bony jaw, a more distinct air of definition, that was totally lacking in Robert's bland, boyish features.

She felt suddenly protective of her old friend. She didn't love him, not in a romantic sense, anyway, but he was as dear to her as her own brother would have been. Besides, she thought, as she marched purposefully over to Robert's side and took his arm, he's available and Blake isn't.

'Blake is working on the building next door to the office,' she explained. 'He very kindly rescued me yesterday when I almost passed out on the street and gave me a ride home.'

'I see,' Robert said through clenched teeth, his tone clearly indicating that he did no such thing.

Blake coughed discreetly. 'I guess I'll take that tour of the garden I mentioned,' he said in a subdued tone of voice. He gave Robert a look of such innocence that Jane longed to slap him. 'I'm trying to talk Jane into doing some landscaping for me,' he said.

'I see,' Robert said again.

Blake looked at Jane. 'Do you mind?' he asked.

She shook her head and watched him as he turned and went out through the kitchen to the garden. When he was out of sight, she looked up at Robert. He was staring fixedly at the spot where Blake had stood, his expression set and angry.

'Would you like some Chinese food?' she asked, moving ahead of him. 'I can warm it up.'

From behind her, she heard his voice calling to her. 'You're not going to work for that man,' he stated flatly.

Slowly, she turned round. 'What did you say?'

He took a step towards her. 'I said I didn't want you to work for Blake Bannister. I know his reputation. His name has been linked with a string of women, and I don't think you should have anything to do with him. Besides, you already have a job.'

This was exactly the conclusion she had come to herself, but somehow hearing it come from Robert in that possessive, dictatorial tone of voice aroused all her resistance.

'Robert,' she said clearly, 'don't use that tone on me.'

'Now, you listen to me, Jane Fairchild,' he said. His voice was rising. 'That man would only mean trouble for a girl like you.'

Jane folded her arms across her chest and glared at him. 'Just what do you mean by that, Robert? "A girl like me". What kind of girl do you think I am?' He opened his mouth to reply, but she wasn't through. 'For your information, Robert,' she went on in a low tone, 'I'm not a girl, I'm a woman, and perfectly well able to make my own decisions about who I choose to work for.'

Robert reached out and grabbed her arm. His face was red, his eyes popping. 'Now, just hold on. Don't get on your high horse with me. I've known you all your life, and I'm telling you right now . . .'

'Let—go—of—me,' she said in a precise, clipped voice. She pulled her arm free and stepped back from him.

She heard Blake's voice, then, coming from behind her. She whirled round to face him. Had he heard the argument with Robert? His expression was bland, and he was smiling pleasantly as he strode into the living-room.

'Well, Jane,' he said. 'I wish you'd reconsider. I'm very impressed with the way you've laid out the garden. It's exactly what I want for my own place. I especially like the fountain and pond set-up. You'd have a free hand, you know, and I'd get my men out to do any necessary construction.'

Jane gave Robert a sidelong glance. Something about the determined set of his chin and the warning look in his eyes irritated her beyond words. With a lift of her chin and a toss of her head, she turned back to Blake.

'All right, Blake,' she said quietly, 'I've changed my mind. I won't promise anything, but I'll at least take a look at it.'

'Good,' he said with satisfaction. His gaze shifted momentarily to the stony-faced Robert. 'I'll call you tomorrow and we can fix up the details,' he said to Jane. 'I'll be on my way now. Nice to have met you, Robert.'

He strode past them then and out of the room. Jane listened to his footsteps, the front door

opening and closing quietly, then the roar of the
motor as he started his car and drove off.

It was only then that she looked at Robert. The
dead silence in the room was resonant with the
waves of hostility and disapproval emanating from
his stolid, motionless form.

'Robert,' she said.

He turned and glared at her. 'Don't say it, Jane.
Don't try to apologise now. It's too late. I warned
you.'

'I had no intention of apologising,' she said
tartly. 'I'd just like you to try to understand.'

'Oh, I understand quite well.' He shook a finger
at her. 'You're playing with fire going anywhere
near a man like Blake Bannister.' He turned on his
heel then and marched out of the house.

Later that evening, Jane sat out in her garden
listening to the gentle patter of water from the
fountain as it fell into the lily pond, and
wondering for the tenth time what in the world
had possessed her to agree to Blake's offer of a
job. It was totally unlike her. She never acted on
impulse. And to quarrel with Robert on top of it!

She still felt a lingering resentment against
Robert. In a way, it was all his fault. She would
never have said yes to Blake, in fact had already
firmly and unequivocally said no, until Robert had
felt called upon to dictate to her like that in such a
heavy-handed fashion. She was sorry to have
quarrelled with her old friend, but really, he was
largely to blame.

Jane knew, sensible, realistic girl that she was,
that the worst kind of deception was self-
deception. She tried always to be ruthlessly honest
about her own motivations, at least to herself.

She couldn't help wondering, then, if in some obscure hidden corner of her mind she had wanted the job with Blake all along and only used Robert's interference as an excuse. If so, my girl, she said to herself, you're in deep trouble. She knew that if there was even a faint hope in her heart or head that the devastating Blake Bannister would come to see her as a desirable woman, she might as well cut her throat right now.

What a difference a day makes, she thought with a sigh. Only yesterday, she had been quite content to watch Blake from a safe distance. In just twenty-four hours, he had managed to march into her life, precipitate a quarrel between her and the man she half thought she might marry, and fill her mind with ideas she'd never dreamed existed.

It was growing cool, and she shivered a little in her thin cotton shirt. She got up to go in the house, her mind still divided between the fear that she had done a very foolish thing and a little thrill of pleasurable anticipation at the knowledge that now she would see him again.

The next day was Friday and, true to his word, Blake called her at the office right after lunch. All morning she had studiously avoided the window where the models gathered to enjoy the view next door. She definitely didn't want the others to find out about her arrangement with him, and was afraid they'd suspect something was up, somehow read it in her face if she caught even a glimpse of him across the way. She could well imagine the endless discussion that would involve, and how could she ever explain it to them? She wasn't quite sure what was going on herself!

'Can you take off early this afternoon?' he asked

without preamble. 'We quit work at three, and I thought we'd drive out to my place so you could get a good look at it while there's plenty of daylight left.'

'I guess so,' she replied slowly.

'Good. I'll meet you out in front at the usual place at three.'

The usual place? That was cute, she thought wryly. He made the scene of her disgrace sound like a rendezvous. She hung up the phone, half-annoyed, half-amused, and, she had to admit, one hundred per cent looking forward to being with him again. She looked up, a secret smile still on her face, to see Randi staring at her speculatively.

'You look like the cat that swallowed the canary,' she commented archly. 'Is Robert back in town?'

'Uh, yes, he is.' No need to explain it hadn't been Robert on the phone.

She dawdled away the next two hours, half-heartedly putting the finishing touches on her June layout. She'd decided to feature old-fashioned roses in the colour spread. They were her great passion in the garden, and she was torn between using the delicate, pale pink Felicite Parmentier, which only bloomed once in the season, and the more flamboyant Madame Isaac Pereire, which flowered repeatedly.

By two-thirty she had decided to use them both, and she spent the next half hour twiddling a pencil in her fingers, trying to look as if she were working, and willing her pounding heart to slow down. Stephanie and Jennifer had gone on to their afternoon appointments with the photographer, and she and Randi were alone in the office.

At five minutes before three, she got up from

her desk, straightened the already neat surface one more time, and started towards the door. The day had dawned warm and sunny, and she hadn't worn a coat that morning. All she needed was her handbag and a notebook.

'I'm leaving now, Randi,' she called on her way out. 'I have an appointment and won't be back.'

Randi glanced up. 'Not the dentist again, I hope.'

'No.' She decided the less said the better and didn't elaborate. 'The stitches don't come out until next week.'

She slipped out of the door before Randi could question her further and walked quickly down the corridor to the bank of lifts. All the way down to the lobby, she had to keep reminding herself that there was nothing personal in this outing with Blake, that she must view it calmly, coolly and professionally as a business meeting.

By the time she stepped off the lift on the main floor and started walking towards the entrance, she was congratulating herself on her success. It helped to get a glimpse of her reflection in the glass door to the street as she approached it, and to see what a businesslike, no-nonsense image she projected, with her sensible heels tapping on the tiled floor, her well-cut navy blue poplin suit, and her clean, plainly styled hair.

But when she saw him out on the pavement, her heart gave its familiar sickening lurch, and she felt her knees begin to buckle. He was standing beside his car, leaning back against it, his slim hips in the worn jeans resting against the bonnet, his arms folded across his chest. His head was turned and lifted slightly as he gazed up at the building under construction, and Jane felt a definite tightening in her throat at the sight of his casual stance, the clean line of his uplifted chin, the strong neck, the dark hair combed neatly and gleaming in the sunshine.

Then his gaze shifted, and the brilliant blue eyes met hers. She made herself keep walking towards him on shaky legs, watching the slow smile of recognition spread across his face as he shoved himself away from the car and stood waiting for her.

'Ah, a prompt woman,' he said, reaching one hand down to open the car door for her. 'I was all prepared to stand out here for another fifteen minutes admiring my building.'

Jane gave him a brief smile. 'Oh, I'm a very efficient person,' she said as she got inside the car. 'It's my one great virtue.'

He came around and got behind the wheel. 'Surely you have more interesting attributes than efficiency,' he said as he slid the car into the lane of traffic. He glanced over at her and winked.

Jane was at a loss for words. She wasn't accustomed to his brand of verbal sparring. That kind of light banter that hovered on the edge of flirtatiousness made her uncomfortable. She decided finally that she didn't need to try to keep up with him. He wanted to hire her to do a job for him. She'd do it on her terms, or she wouldn't do it at all.

She gazed evenly at him, then almost faltered at the sight of that near-perfect profile. She collected herself instantly and looked away. Surely, she thought, with practice it will get easier to quit turning to jelly every time I look at him. Try to think of him as a rose bush. Alfred de Dalmas, perhaps, or Jacques Cartier. Breathtaking to look at, but full of thorns.

'Let's just stick to efficiency,' she said at last, 'it's what you'll be paying me for. Tell me a little about the property and what you want to do with it.'

They were crossing Mercer Island now, heading for the East Channel bridge and the mountains of the Cascade range, which still sparkled with snow, even in May. To the north, the pristine peak of Mount Baker rose up against the blue sky. To the south, only the very tip of Mount Rainier was visible, its lower portion blanketed in mist.

'I have six acres,' he said, 'and I want to leave most of it in woods. There's a clearing around the house, maybe one acre in all, with a natural pond and the small creek that feeds it. I've left all the native dogwoods standing, and I'd like to build the garden around them.' He glanced at her. 'What do you think?'

She nodded. 'That's a good idea. There are probably lots of native plants in the surrounding woods you can dig up and replant. It's a little late now, but you can still plant rhododendrons and azaleas. Are you interested in growing flowers, or do you want a strictly low-maintenance garden?'

'Oh, I won't be doing any of the gardening myself,' he said. 'I'll have that done.'

'But that's half the fun!' she exclaimed. 'Planting things and tending them yourself and watching them develop.'

He shook his head. 'Can't do it, I'm afraid. I travel in my job. Sometimes I'm gone for weeks at a time.'

'I thought Bannister Construction was a local firm.'

'It is, but I'm an ambitious type. I'm bidding on a job in Houston right now.'

They were passing through the small town of North Bend, the last civilisation until Snoqualmie Pass at the summit, when suddenly a car came out of a side street directly towards them. With instant reflexes, Blake twisted the wheel and swerved into the next lane, throwing Jane heavily against him in the process.

His arm shot out around her, holding her steady. 'Damn fool driver,' he muttered. 'Are you OK?'

'Yes, I'm fine.' She was a little shaken, but not by the near-accident. The feel of the strongly muscled arm that held her round her shoulders, the large hand that gripped her arm, the hard chest under her head, all created a turmoil within her that she had to struggle to control.

They came to the Fall City turn-off shortly, and he casually removed his arm to take the sharp left off the highway, allowing Jane to move unobtrusively over to her side of the seat. They drove in silence down the narrow two-lane road until they came to a chainlink fence with an open gate in the centre.

They were in the mountains now, or at least in the high foothills, and through the open window of the car Jane could sense the difference from the city in the cooler fresher air, the faint tang of cedar and pine, the rustling branches of the maples and birches, and the peaceful stillness.

They drove in through the gate along the freshly paved road that wound around the native trees and shrubs until it came to a rough clearing, and Jane caught her first sight of Blake's house.

She caught her breath at the beauty of it, but beauty was too weak a word, she thought. There was such a sense of absolute *rightness* about the low sprawling structure that made it look as though it had grown up there naturally. It was finished with rough cedar boarding and was set on a low knoll at the top of a rise where the land fell away gradually on the far side of it.

The native dogwoods were in full white flower, and immediately a hundred different ways to put in a garden popped into Jane's head, possibilities that would enhance the natural setting to the full rather than compete with it. As they drove slowly along, she literally hung out of the window, making rapid mental calculations of footage and terrain for later design.

Finally she turned to Blake, her eyes shining with sheer joy. He was watching her very intently, a thoughtful look on his face, but she was too excited to wonder what was behind the penetrating blue gaze.

'Blake, it's beautiful!' she breathed.

He smiled then. 'Think you want to tackle the job, then?'

'Try and stop me. If I weren't such a practical person, I'd do it for nothing. But since you've offered to pay me . . .'

They both started laughing, then, but when she turned to look out of the window again, the laughter died in her throat as she saw a bright yellow sports car parked in front of the house and a tall, dark-haired woman walking down the steps of the wide porch towards them.

Blake stopped the car and got out. Jane sat there for a moment, her pleasure in the lovely setting marred somewhat by the jarring note of the garish car, and the appearance of Monica Mason. She had recognised her instantly. It seemed as though her photograph appeared weekly in the newspaper at one grand social event after another, and *Northwest Life Magazine* had run a pictorial interview with her last year.

She watched now as Blake strode towards her. When they met, he held her loosely by the waist, and she reached her arms up around his neck. She was a tall woman, but even so, he had to bend down to kiss her lightly on the mouth. It wasn't a lover's kiss—no more, really, than the friendly pecks she had exchanged with Robert—but still it bothered her, even though they broke apart immediately.

Come on, now, she admonished herself, cut that out. She had known he was engaged to Monica Mason all along and, even if she had conveniently forgotten that fact, she had realised from the beginning that Blake Bannister was out of bounds for her. Think about the job, she told herself sternly. That's why you're here.

She heard Blake calling to her, then, and she got out of the car. Squaring her shoulders and smoothing out her skirt, she walked towards them. As she came closer, she had to admit that Monica Mason was a real beauty, far lovelier than her photographs had revealed her to be. She had a very finished, polished look, with her smooth raven hair, perfect complexion and a figure that filled her cream-coloured raw-silk trousers and casual shirt as though she'd been born in them.

'Jane, this is Monica Mason. Monica, Jane Fairchild. I've talked her into planning the garden for me,' he explained to Monica.

Jane smiled. 'How do you do,' she said quietly.

She was immediately aware that the other woman was assessing her, appraising her, almost as though trying to decide whether to consider her a potential rival or one of the hired help. The cool green-eyed gaze was in no way rude or even challenging, but Jane knew for certain that she was being judged in some way.

Finally, as though she had made up her mind at last, Monica smiled back at Jane and held out a hand.

'It's nice to meet you,' she said. Her voice was low and melodious with a cultivated accent that spoke of the best schools. 'Blake has been dying to get the garden in ever since the house was finished, and neither one of us knows the first thing about it.'

She made her ignorance of horticulture sound like a virtue, Jane thought, or at least a mark of distinction, as though such crude interests were beneath a really cultivated person. Jane only smiled again.

'Well,' she said, 'I guess we all have our own areas of interest.' She turned to Blake. 'I'd like to take some measurements first,' she said in a businesslike tone. She felt calm and competent with the thought of getting to work at something she knew she could do well. 'Do you have a long tape measure I can use?'

'Sure,' he said, 'I'll go get it. But can you work in those clothes?'

'Oh, yes, no problem. I'm not going to do any digging, after all. I just want to walk around for a while and get the feel of the place.'

'Well,' he said, 'I can help you with the measurements. It takes two, you know, to get an accurate fix. One to hold the tape in place, the other to do the pacing.'

'That won't be necessary,' she said firmly. 'Actually, I can just pace it off roughly today anyway without a tape. Just give me a few hours, and I'll have a rough sketch. I can come back some other time if I need more precise measurements.'

'Well, OK,' he said dubiously, 'but I'll do the pacing off. I'm dressed for it.' He glanced down at his heavy work boots.

Monica sighed dramatically. 'Honestly, darling, those awful clothes!' She gave Jane a look of feminine complicity. 'Can you tell me why a man who would never have to work another day in his life chooses to dress up like a—a day labourer?' She wrinkled her perfect nose and fluttered her long eyelashes at Blake. 'Look at you!' she exclaimed. 'You're filthy.' Then she smiled indulgently and took him by the arm. 'Why don't you let Miss Fairchild get on with her work by herself while you go clean up?'

Jane could see by the stubborn set of Blake's jaw that he was about to object to Monica's plan. For some reason, she realised with surprise, he wants to help me, most likely because he's not a man who would take kindly to any kind of dictation, even from the lovely Monica.

'That's a good idea,' she put in hurriedly. She took her notebook and pencil out of her bag. 'I work better alone, anyway.'

She turned, then, and walked away from them before Blake could voice the objection she knew was on the tip of his tongue. She didn't look back.

As she worked, pacing off distances, making sketches, jotting down rough measurements, Jane became so immersed in what she was doing and so entranced with the possibilities offered by the beautiful piece of property, that she lost all track of time. It was hot work, and eventually she had to take off her jacket and roll up the sleeves of her blouse. She wished she'd worn more suitable clothes, but she could come out on her own another time to do a more thorough job.

She had gone far along a narrow dirt path into the woods below the driveway to look at the native plants and see if she might be able to use some in her plan, when she heard the sudden roar of a motor. She looked up to see the little yellow car streaking by in a cloud of dust, a stony-faced Monica at the wheel. Jane half raised a hand politely to wave goodbye, but the car had sped past by then, and without a glance her way from Monica.

Jane shrugged and continued her search. After a while, she became aware of a shadow looming across her field of vision, and she turned around to see Blake standing at the top of the rise, his long legs apart, his knuckles resting on his slim hips.

The sun was beginning to lower in the western sky, and its brilliant glow fell directly on him. He had obviously showered and changed his clothes. He was dressed in a clean pair of jeans, a pair of gleaming leather boots and a clean white shirt with the sleeves rolled up. He looked dazzling.

'Do you realise you've been out here for two hours?' he asked. He held out a hand. 'Come on, it's quitting time. I'll fix you some dinner, and then I'll take you home.'

She glanced at the hand beckoning to her. Without thinking what she was doing, she started walking slowly up the rise towards him, then took his outstretched hand and allowed him to help her up the last few steps until she stood beside him.

'Look at you,' he said with mock sternness. 'For

such a neat lady, always so well put together, you're a mess.'

Jane looked down at her rumpled blue skirt and dust-covered pumps. 'It's all right,' she said. 'I can't work unless I get dirty. It's half the fun of gardening.' She brushed off her skirt. 'It'll wash out anyway.'

'Ah, a woman after my own heart,' he said. 'Come on. I want to show you the house.'

CHAPTER FIVE

THEY ate their light supper out on the large wooden veranda at the back of the house just off the kitchen. It was very peaceful and quiet, and Jane mused that she had never been in a strange place before where she'd felt so much at home. The creek running across Blake's property was only about fifty feet from the house, and they could hear the babbling of the water, the croaking of the frogs in the pond and the whisper of the soft evening breeze in the tall evergreens.

It was a far better meal than she had anticipated, a delicious casserole with herbs and mushrooms and chunks of meat cooked in a wine sauce, and she complimented Blake on his culinary expertise.

He was leaning casually back in his chair. The sun had just set, and Jane watched the evening shadows playing about his fine features. If only he weren't so heartbreakingly beautiful, she thought, and wondered once again if she hadn't been foolish to take a job that would put her in such close contact with him.

'I'm afraid I can't take any credit for the meal,' he said. 'A local woman comes in every day to cook and clean for me.'

'You shouldn't have disillusioned me,' she said with a smile. 'Although you do open a mean can of soup.'

He inclined his head, accepting the compliment. 'I do at that, don't I?' He lit a slim brown cheroot. 'I take it you've decided to accept the job.'

'Yes, of course,' she said. 'I'm looking forward to it, but I do feel a little guilty about taking money for something that will be such fun.'

'I'm sure you'll earn it,' he said, 'and it's well worth it to me. I'm going to be out of town for a few weeks, and want you to feel free to come out here any time you need to. The gate is always open, or at least unlocked.'

Jane wondered if his trip out of town was the reason for Monica's hasty departure. He'd said over dinner that she objected to his travelling.

As though able to read her mind, he chuckled deep in his throat and said, 'Monica wasn't pleased, as you no doubt noticed. She's not usually so rude. She has impeccable manners.' The way he said it, it didn't sound as though he placed an exceptionally high value on such a virtue.

'She's very lovely,' Jane murmured.

'Yes,' he agreed, 'she is that.'

Jane longed to ask him when they planned to be married, but decided it was better to keep their whole relationship on as professional and impersonal a plane as possible. With that in mind, she stood up and reached for her jacket, draped over the back of her chair.

'It's getting late,' she said. 'It's too bad you have to drive me all the way back to Mercer Island. We should have stopped and picked up my car.'

He crushed out his cigar in the heavy glass ashtray on the table and stood up. 'No trouble at all. Monica lives in Windermere. I'll go on into town to her place and see if I can mend some fences.'

He stretched widely, raising his arms high above

his head and flexing his shoulder muscles. As he
did so, the fine white material of his shirt was
stretched to outline the near-perfect symmetry of
his upper torso, and the jeans hung lower on his
lean hips. Jane looked away, just as he tucked in
his shirt, warning herself once again to close her
mind firmly to any personal thoughts about him.

During the next few days, Jane's life settled back
into its familiar pattern. She'd only really known
Blake for a few days, not long enough to get
seriously attached to him or think of him as a part
of her life. Their brief acquaintance had happened
so fast and under such odd circumstances that
now, in his absence, the whole thing began to take
on the cloudy aspect of a dream.

She'd made up her quarrel with Robert, too, in
the meantime, and they were back on their old
friendly footing. She still hadn't made up her mind
about marrying him, and he seemed to accept her
hesitation much more gracefully once she'd
convinced him that Blake Bannister had nothing
to do with it.

It was all for the best, she thought the
following Friday night as she worked on the plans
for Blake's garden. It was an interesting project,
and she was able to detach it from the man himself
so that that's all it was. He'd been gone a week,
and she wanted to have some progress made
before he returned. After all, he was paying her for
a job and, as her employer, he had a right to
expect results.

She sat at the dining-room table, where she liked
to work, and drew a sketch of Blake's house and
the surrounding property from the rough
measurements she'd taken the previous week when

he'd taken her out there. As she worked, she realised she'd have to go back to get a more accurate fix on certain areas she'd only been able to rough in that day. Maybe she'd drive out tomorrow, she thought. He'd be gone for another week, and the sensible thing would be to go when she knew he wouldn't be there.

She had gone as far as she could with the measurements she had, and she looked down at the sketch she'd just completed with a real glow of satisfaction. Ideas had come to her for various planting possibilities as she worked, a clump of rhododendrons here, a blaze of bright deciduous azaleas there, a pink dogwood, some hardy lilies for the pond, and she started listing them in her notebook for future reference.

Just then the doorbell rang. She glanced at her watch. It was past nine o'clock. She'd been working on the plans for two hours. I really should keep track of my time, she thought, as she went through the living-room to the front door, since Blake was paying her by the hour.

In the front hall, she hesitated before opening the door. Living alone in the house, she was a little wary about intruders. Still, it wasn't quite dark out, the neighbours were within calling distance, and she didn't really think a burglar or a rapist would ring the doorbell. Besides, she could keep the chain on. It was probably Robert, although he usually called before he came over, or the paper boy collecting. It was almost the first of June.

The bell rang again, and she opened the door the few inches allowed by the chain to see Blake Bannister standing there under the porch light. She could only stare. He was dressed in a well-cut navy blue blazer, dark grey trousers and a white shirt open at the neck.

'What are you doing here?' she finally managed to ask.

'Are you going to make your employer stand out here all night?' he asked with a lift of his dark eyebrows.

The sight of him took her breath away. She had forgotten how devastatingly attractive, how totally masculine he was. He looked taller in the more formal clothes, more impressive, even more dangerous, and, she thought sadly, more unattainable.

As she released the chain lock and opened the door wider, she hastily reminded herself of that fact, and by the time he was inside, with the door closed behind him, she had sensibly collected herself.

'I didn't mean to send you into a tailspin,' he said, looking down at her with amusement in the blue eyes.

'I never go into tailspins,' she said firmly, 'I just wasn't expecting you.' She led the way into the living-room. 'I thought you'd be gone another week.'

'So did I,' he said, following her. 'Houston was too hot, though, and I managed to accomplish all I needed to in a week.'

He took off his jacket and draped it over a chair, then unbuttoned his shirtsleeves and rolled them up twice.

'Make yourself at home,' she murmured.

'Thanks,' he said, sauntering into the adjoining dining-room. He flashed her a smile. 'I will.'

As she watched him standing at the dining-room table surveying the plans she had been working on,

she became uncomfortably conscious of her own
appearance. Although she made it a point of pride
never to dress really sloppily, she was acutely
aware that the casual, simply styled cotton
sundress was not exactly the height of fashion. Her
flat-heeled sandals and bare legs didn't help. With
a little twinge of guilt, she thought of the flesh-
coloured teddy she wore underneath the dress. Her
penchant for filmy lingerie had never bothered her
near Robert. Why, then, should it affect her this
way near Blake?

He was still studying the drawing, and she began
to grow angry with herself for allowing his
presence in her house to muddle her thinking the
way it did. Summoning up all her resources, she
sternly admonished herself to shape up. He'd just
surprised her, that's all, taken her off guard. He
seemed to be very good at that.

'Well,' she said, coming up to stand beside him,
'what do you think?'

He glanced over at her. 'I don't know what I
think,' he said with a lift of his broad shoulders.
'Remember, I'm a horticultural moron, that's why
I hired you. Why don't you explain it to me?'

'It's still very rough,' she said. She reached in
front of him to point out certain landmarks she'd
sketched in. 'You see, here's the pond and this is
the path through the woods. I thought a clump of
rhodies here, and maybe some native plants to fill
in over there.'

As she went on to elaborate on her ideas, she
became so engrossed in the plan that she could
almost forget his disturbing presence. Then,
suddenly, he leaned down to examine a detail
of the plan more closely, and spoke for the first
time.

'How about here?' he asked, pointing. 'Up against the house.'

She turned to him to reply, but the words died on her lips when she saw that his face was only inches away from hers. He was still gazing intently down at the plan of the table, and for a moment, she stared at him, speechless.

They were so close that she could see the faint stubble on his jaw and chin, the tiny lines around his downcast eyes, the way his black hair fell in a smooth wave over his forehead and curled around his ear, the long dark lashes resting on his high, sharply etched cheekbones.

Then, suddenly, his gaze shifted towards her, and for one second the bright blue eyes held her in a near-hypnotised state. She jerked her head upright, as though she'd been burned, and made herself move a few inches away from him.

'As you can see,' she said huskily, 'it's very rough.' She couldn't look at him. 'But you can probably get the general idea.'

When she sensed that he had straightened up beside her, she looked at him. He was gazing intently at her, a slightly puzzled, almost questioning look on his face, as though mulling something over in his mind. All she could think of was that he didn't like the plan.

'If you don't approve,' she said hastily, 'I can always change it around to suit you. These are my ideas, remember, but it's going to be *your* garden. You're the one who has the final say.'

'Oh, the plan is fine,' he said with an offhand motion of his hand. 'I trust your judgment.' He frowned down at his feet for a moment, then smiled at her. 'Do you suppose I could have a drink?'

'A drink?' She was momentarily nonplussed. 'I'm not sure I have anything.' Then she recalled that her father had kept a supply of liquor for entertaining tucked away in the kitchen cupboard. 'Yes,' she said. 'What would you like?'

'Do you have any Scotch?'

'I think so. I'll have to look.'

He followed her into the kitchen, stopping along the way to inspect the framed floral watercolours hung on one wall of the dining-room.

'I like these,' he called after her. 'Did you do them?'

'Yes,' she called back to him from the kitchen. The liquor was in the highest cupboard, and she pulled the stool over to climb on so she could reach it. 'It's a hobby of mine.'

'They're quite good,' he said, walking towards her and looking up at her perched precariously on top of the stool. 'You should have let me do that,' he said.

She found the bottle of Scotch and leaned over to set it down on the worktop. He was standing behind her holding on to the stool to keep it steady. Suddenly, as she looked down, she experienced a slight attack of vertigo, a momentary wave of dizziness, and to her horror, she felt herself losing her footing.

The next thing she knew, his arms had come round her from behind, holding her firmly and breaking her fall. He pulled her bodily off the stool and finally, gratefully, she felt the firm ground under her feet.

At the same time, she felt a large hand planted squarely on her breast as he helped her steady herself. She knew it was an accident, that it had happened only in the confusion of the moment, but nonetheless, the touch of his hand over the thin cotton sundress set up a clamouring in her very being so powerful that another attack of vertigo threatened and she slumped weakly back against his long, hard body.

What is happening to me? she thought wildly, as blind sensation took over and sent her good sense out the window. He was standing very still, absolutely motionless, and she herself stood as though rooted to the spot. The very air seemed to be filled with a crackling of electrical tension. It was as though time had stood still.

Then, at the same moment, she felt the hand on her breast move slightly and his soft breath on her neck as he bent down to place his lips there. She turned her head, inexorably, blindly drawn towards the mouth that was doing such wonderful things to the nape of her neck.

'Jane,' he breathed into her ear, and his hand moved slowly across to her other breast.

Drowning in the overpowering sensations his touch had sent surging through her, she let her head drop back further on to his broad chest and closed her eyes with a sigh.

Then his mouth was on hers in a searing kiss that left her breathless with wonder. His lips moved tantasingly on hers, opening now to tug gently at her mouth, running his tongue over it. His other hand slid up from her waist, brushing over her other breast and settling around the bare flesh of her throat.

Finally, when she didn't think she could bear another moment of the powerful reaction he was evoking in her, he lifted his head. He put his hands on her shoulders and turned her round so that he was looking down at her. She swallowed hard, then opened her eyes to meet that blue gaze.

'I think we'd better talk,' he said softly.

She nodded and backed away from him a step. He dropped his hands from her shoulders, then turned and took hold of the bottle of Scotch. He held it up with an enquiring look. Still dazed, she shook her head and reached up in the cupboard for glasses. She went to the refrigerator, took out a bottle of white wine and poured herself a glass while he fixed his drink.

He rested his lean hips back on the worktop, his long legs crossed in front of him, and took a long swallow of Scotch and water. As she sipped her wine, she watched him carefully and felt her senses gradually settle down to near normal. She wasn't quite sure yet just what had happened there a few moments ago, but she did know it was probably the one most enjoyable moment of her life, and she wasn't going to spoil it with vain regrets.

She wasn't sorry it had happened, but she knew it would never happen again, and she intended to savour the precious moment. She had no idea what had got into Blake. She'd been so certain he'd never thought of her that way, and doubted very much if he did now. They'd both been caught unawares by the propinquity of the moment, that was all, and she searched her mind calmly for some way to let him off the hook gracefully, to let him know she attached no significance to it, when he finally spoke.

'I was hoping that would happen,' he said quietly.

She gave him a long slow look. 'I don't understand,' she said at last.

'I've been wanting to do that since the first time you fell into my arms, a couple of months ago on Fat Tuesday.'

Her eyes widened in disbelief. Then she smiled. 'I can hardly believe that,' she said.

'Why do you put yourself down?' he said gruffly. His voice had an almost angry tone.

'Oh, I'm not,' she replied easily. 'I know myself quite well, pluses as well as minuses. I don't feel inferior at all, but I certainly know my limitations, and sex object I'm not.'

He eyed her carefully. 'You really believe that?'

She laughed and took another sip of wine. 'I *know* that, Blake, but it's never really mattered to me. There are other things in life, you know.'

'What about Robert?'

'Oh, Robert,' she said with a wave of her hand. 'We're old, old friends. Robert's at a time in his life when he's beginning to think about settling down, raising a family. I'm the only woman he really knows well, so he decided he was in love with me and wanted to marry me.'

'Are you going to marry him?'

She shook her head slowly from side to side. 'No,' she said, 'I'm not. Funny, I don't think I realised it until just this minute, but it would be wrong to marry Robert. He's a wonderful man, and I hope we'll always be friends, but he deserves someone who's really in love with him.'

He nodded. 'And what about you. Don't you want to marry? Have a family?'

'I used to think I did, but now I'm not so sure. I was never in love with Robert, but I just assumed we would drift into marriage some day. That is, until he started talking about it. Then I knew I couldn't do it.' She eyed him thoughtfully. 'How about you? You're going to marry Monica Mason, aren't you?'

'I'm like you, I used to think so. Our families are old friends, and, like you and Robert, it was always assumed we'd marry. But that's all off. She doesn't want a man who gets his hands dirty, and I've come to realise that the way I live, travelling so much, doesn't make for good husband material.'

'I'm sorry,' she murmured, thinking that if she'd been Monica Mason she would have followed this man to the ends of the earth if that's where he wanted to go.

He held up a hand. 'Don't be. We had it out last Friday after I brought you home. It had been brewing for a long time. I got tired of apologising for what I do, who I am, and broke it off.' He poured himself another drink.

As they'd been talking, Jane had experienced the odd sensation that she was split in two. One part of her mind listened, spoke, participated in the conversation. The other was firmly fixed on the brief moment they'd shared. She could still taste his mouth on hers, remember the feel of his hand on her breast, the hard strength of his arms and body as he held her.

Listening to him now, she wondered what he was leading up to with this calm discussion of their respective relationships with Monica and Robert, or if he was leading up to anything at all. He'd said they needed to talk. Well, they were talking, but it didn't seem to her that they were getting anywhere.

He was still speaking in a low, steady voice, telling her now about his love of building things, how he'd always been fascinated as a boy with

construction sets, spending hours at a time
absorbed in constructing intricate buildings and
machines.

But, as she watched him, she only listened with
half an ear. What really held her attention was the
man himself. She heard the words coming from his
mouth, but it was the movement of the fine
chiselled lips that riveted her gaze, and the way he
held his glass in his large, well-shaped hands or
gestured to make a point, the muscular forearms,
the silky black hairs sprinkled over the tanned
skin; all interested her far more than the substance
of his speech.

She felt as though she could spend the rest of
her life just looking at him, but beneath this
fascination with his physical beauty, her habitual
common sense was slowly beginning to assert
itself.

She tore her eyes away from the mobile mouth,
the competent-looking hands, the lithe graceful
body, and forced herself to pay closer attention to
what he was saying. When he did get round to the
point he was making with regard to their
relationship, she wanted to be well prepared with a
sound, practical view of her own. She'd never
known a man who could turn her normally sane
thought processes upside down as this one could,
with just a touch, a word, a look; and she told
herself firmly, it's got to stop.

'So you see,' he said, 'I've pretty much given up
the idea of marrying, settling down, raising a
family. Those are fine things, but they just don't fit
into my scheme of things, my work, at the
moment; and for me, my work is everything.'

She was really paying attention now. Was this
his point? Was he telling her to forget any ideas

she might have about a serious relationship with him or any kind of a future based on that one brief kiss? She set her wine glass down carefully on the kitchen worktop and gave him a steady, direct look.

'That's all very interesting,' she said quietly, 'but I don't see what it has to do with me.' She smiled. 'If you're warning me off any plans I might be making to trap you into marriage based on one kiss, it really isn't necessary.'

The blue eyes widened and a slow flush began to spread over his face. 'You're a pretty direct lady, aren't you?' He took a swallow of Scotch.

'I try to be,' she said calmly. 'It saves a lot of misunderstanding.'

'I must have sounded pretty arrogant,' he said apologetically. 'I know I said it badly, and I had no intention of "warning you off". I just wanted to be honest with you, to get my thinking across, all up front, before we got involved with each other.'

She put the cork back in the bottle of wine and replaced it on the shelf in the refrigerator. Then she stood before him with her arms across in front of her.

'Involved, Blake?' she asked. 'We're not "involved", and I see no way we're going to be in the future. I work for you, you're paying me to do a job for you. That's all.'

The blue eyes narrowed at her. 'Are you trying to tell me that kiss meant nothing to you? Or that you don't want to take it further? Because if you are, Miss Fairchild, I'm going to have to call you a liar.'

She could sense the barely suppressed anger underlying his words. A man like Blake Bannister doesn't get turned down every day of the week, she thought, and watching him now she could well understand why not. She was still sorely tempted, especially now that he'd made it clear he just assumed they would enter into an affair.

What an experience that would be to look back on and reminisce about in her old age! But she knew now absolutely that, for her, it would never work, and she had to make him understand that without wounding his male vanity more than she already had.

'Blake, try to understand. I don't know the first thing about playing games with a man. All I can do is to be absolutely honest with you and tell you exactly what's on my mind.' She frowned and bit her lip, not quite sure how to proceed.

'I'm waiting,' he said impatiently after a few moments.

She gazed levelly at him. 'First of all, I must tell you quite frankly—and at the risk of contributing to your vanity—that you are without a doubt the most attractive man I've ever known. I love the way you look, the way you move and talk, even the way you think.' She paused and frowned as she searched her mind for the right words to express what she felt.

'Go on,' Blake prompted. 'That's all very flattering, but I'm still mystified. If that's what you think of me, why are you backing off from an involvement?'

'Well, you see,' she said, spreading her arms wide, 'that's just the point. It's *because* I think you're so attractive and because of the way you make me feel that I won't take one step in that direction. I'm uncomfortable with it.' She shook her head. 'No, I'm *terrified* of it. I have a strong intuition that it would do me harm, even irreparable harm, to fall in love with you.'

'Love?' he asked with some surprise. 'I'm not asking you to fall in love with me, for God's sake. I'm not talking about love.'

'Oh? What, then? What are you talking about? Just good old plain unvarnished sex?'

He flushed again. 'You do have a way of putting things bluntly,' he murmured. He shoved his hands in his trouser pockets and began to pace around the kitchen. 'No,' he said at last, 'I'm not talking about sex, not the way you mean. Hell, I like you, Jane. I like being with you. I also find you very attractive physically. Is there something wrong with that?'

She had to laugh at that. 'Me!' she exclaimed, pointing at her chest. 'Listen, Blake, I've been plain Jane all my life. After a beautiful woman like Monica Mason, I'm probably a novelty to you, that's all. There's nothing remotely glamorous or sexy about me, and we both know it.'

He stood before her now, eyeing her speculatively. 'No,' he said slowly, 'you're not glamorous, but whoever told you you weren't sexy must have been either out of his mind or senile or blind.' He reached out a hand and run it lightly over her face. 'I love the way you look. You've got good strong bones, lovely brown eyes, a very kissable mouth. You've got character in your face.' He smoothed her hair back from her forehead. 'Beautiful thick hair the colour of ripe chestnuts.' He bent his head to put it against hers. 'I love the way it smells, so fresh and clean.'

Jane was turning hot, then cold, then hot again. His mouth was on her hair now, and she could feel his breath ruffling it as he spoke.

'Blake,' she said in a strangled voice.

'And underneath the prim clothes you wear,' he crooned on, ignoring her, 'is a body any sex goddess would be proud of.'

His hands were on her shoulders now and moving gently over her upper arms, brushing against the sides of her breasts. She felt his mouth leave her hair, linger for a moment on her forehead, her nose, her cheeks, until finally it was tugging gently on her upper lip.

Her breath was coming in short little gasps now, and her lips parted involuntarily in a purely reflexive action under his seeking, insistent mouth, which opened now to take possession of her in a searing kiss that she could no more have refused to respond to than she could fly. When she felt his hot tongue invade the inside of her mouth, searching and probing, her knees almost buckled under her, and she slumped weakly against his chest, clutching the strong hard muscles of his arms to keep from falling.

The kiss went on and on, the mobile mouth seeking out her deepest secrets, and now his hands moved slowly over her straining breasts, down her ribcage and round to hold her firmly by the hips. As he pulled her lower body tightly up against his, she could feel the full force of his hard arousal, and this evidence of her power over him made her head spin wildly.

Then she heard him groan deep in his throat. He tore his mouth away from hers and brought his arms up around her back to hold her closely to him. He put his mouth at her ear then and spoke in a low, urgent voice.

'God, I want you, Jane,' he breathed. 'My little brown girl.' He stroked her back, her hips, her waist, then one hand came around to her breast and slipped inside the front opening of her dress.

At the first touch of his fingers on her erect, aching nipple, Jane was suddenly acutely conscious that she stood at a crossroads. In spite of the waves of sensuous pleasure his touch on her bare flesh awakened in her, and the yearning she felt in her loins, she could still barely think. And what she thought, in that one brief moment of clarity, was that if she allowed him to go on, as she knew she longed for him to do, she would be lost, her life would be shattered, and all for a pleasure that, however intense, was fleeting, had no future.

It was the single most agonising decision she'd ever had to make in her life, but her years of self-control and integrity came to help her, and she did it. With a low moan of pain, she pushed at Blake's chest with all her might, propelling herself out of his embrace, and backed away from him in short, staggering steps.

She couldn't look at him. She was so afraid to meet that blue gaze that she whirled around and braced herself against the worktop, still panting. She hung her head, struggling to collect herself, to regain control of her shattered emotions, and felt both grateful and disappointed at the same time that he made no movement towards her, nor did he utter a word.

Finally, she raised her head and, without turning round, said in a voice that still shook, 'I want you to leave now, Blake.'

'Jane,' he said, and she heard him take a step towards her.

She turned then and looked at him. His face was haggard, the blue eyes clouded with bewilderment, the black hair tousled and falling over his

forehead. It was all she could do to keep from
running across the few feet that separated them
and throwing herself into his arms.

'Please,' she begged, close to tears now. 'Please
go.'

He opened his mouth and raised a hand towards
her, but when she lifted her chin firmly and gave
him a defiant look, he clamped his lips shut and
dropped his hand. Then he turned around and
strode out of the room.

She stood at the worktop motionless, her hands
gripping the edge of it so hard that her knuckles
were white. She heard his footsteps as he went into
the living-room to retrieve his jacket, then down
the hall to the front door.

When she heard the door open, then close
behind him, she let go at last. With a strangled cry,
she buried her face in her hands and sobbed.

She made up her mind later that night as she lay
staring blankly up at the ceiling of her bedroom
that she would never look back. She saw now that
she'd been reacting and behaving like a silly
adolescent ever since the first night she'd met him
down in Pioneer Square. It was totally out of
character for her, and she'd been right to put a
stop to it before it got really out of hand.

From the moment he'd come into her life, Blake
Bannister had turned it upside down. He'd swept
her away like a powerful tide, just by the sheer
force of his personality and good looks. She'd
quarrelled with Robert, neglected her job on the
magazine, spent most of her time mooning over a
man who was out of her reach, and almost got
herself involved in an affair with him that would
have destroyed her.

Yet, as she tossed and turned, she knew she still desired him, still wanted him, more than she'd ever wanted anything in her life. Even now, an insidious little inner voice kept whispering to her that it would have been worth it. She would have been hurt eventually, of course, but maybe . . .

No! she told herself firmly. She knew she'd done the right thing. Besides, it was too late now anyway. A man like Blake Bannister wouldn't take kindly to rejection from any woman, much less plain Jane.

That should give me some satisfaction, she told herself in the darkness, to have been the one to call it off even before it had begun. But somehow the thought was cold comfort. It didn't help at all to allay the aching, throbbing void in her heart.

CHAPTER SIX

As the weeks passed and Jane picked up the threads of her life again, the whole episode with Blake Bannister came to seem to her like a dream. He had come crashing into her safe little world like a tropical hurricane, then, just as suddenly, he was gone. The very next day, she had burned the few sketches and notes she'd made of his proposed garden, and resolutely vowed to put all thoughts of him out of her mind. She even stayed religiously away from the window at the office, just in case she might catch a glimpse of his working on the building next door.

She wanted no reminders of him at all to tempt her back into that awful condition of slavery she'd been in such danger of falling into in their brief encounter. She hated that feeling and, as time passed, she vaguely blamed him for taking advantage of her. He was so sure of himself, so aware of his enormous appeal, that he must surely have believed this particular plain Jane would be a pushover, an easy conquest to add to his undoubtedly long list.

This simmering resentment she cultivated deliberately helped her over the worst of missing him. Each time she was tempted to dwell on how his kisses had made her feel, or the sheer bliss of being in his arms, or even the way he looked and spoke and moved, she would remind herself that he had only been playing a game with her.

It gave her a lot of satisfaction, too, that she had

been the one to send him away, to break it off before it got started. And, she told herself finally, even if he had been telling her the truth when he'd said he really liked her, was attracted to her, he'd also made it quite clear that he wasn't interested in a permanent relationship with any woman.

Her relationship with Robert continued on the old terms now that Robert had dropped his pose of outraged lover. He hadn't pressed her for an answer to his proposal, but at times he would make oblique references to the future in a way that seemed to assume they would spend it together.

She never objected when he did this. What was the use? She hadn't agreed to marry him, and, if the time ever came that he should bring the issue out in the open, she could still back out. As time went on, however, she began to think that probably she would just drift into marriage with him eventually, if only out of inertia.

This thought depressed her profoundly whenever it struck her. Was that what she wanted? He'd make an ideal husband for her. He'd give her all the freedom she needed for her own work. He'd be faithful to her, she knew, given his apparently low level of sexual needs. If they ever decided to have children, he'd be a wonderful father. He had a good stable job and was doing quite well in his law firm. What was wrong with him—or with her— that she didn't jump at the chance he offered?

It was then that the little voice would begin to whisper to her. *He's not Blake Bannister*, it said, *that's what's wrong with him*.

In July, Seattle enjoyed one of its rare heatwaves. The temperature soared up into the high nineties and just hung there for a solid week.

Women appeared on the city streets in the most outlandishly skimpy outfits, and all anyone seemed able to talk about was the weather. Instead of saying, 'How are you?' when they met, people had begun greeting each other now with, 'Hot enough for you?'

The work on the building next door seemed to have come to a screeching halt, with rumours of further strikes and, Jane heard from the disappointed models, mysterious delays in shipments of material. Jane was not fond of hot weather, and at least she didn't have to endure the added annoyance of all that racket across the way.

On a blistering Monday morning, however, she entered her office to the tune of hammering metal, whining saws and clanking, grinding machinery. It was almost ninety degrees outside already at ten o'clock in the morning, and the weatherman had confidently predicted the temperature would reach one hundred by mid-afternoon, a real rarity for Seattle residents.

Jane had worn her coolest dress, a lightweight sleeveless cotton with a scooped neck, but even so she felt sticky and wilted by the time she got to work, just from walking the few blocks from where she'd parked her car.

To add to the construction noise, the models were clustered again at the window in their strapless sundresses, squealing and giggling and obviously overjoyed that work had begun again. Jane listened to them as she crossed over to her desk, wondering crossly how grown women could make such fools of themselves over men and congratulating herself once again on her own narrow escape and more sensible view of the other sex.

'Ohhh,' Jennifer was sighing dramatically. 'Here comes the blond Viking!'

'He's gorgeous,' Stephanie admitted, 'but take a look at the Latin-looking one in the black trousers. That smouldering Spanish type really turns me on.'

'Yes, but look at the shoulders on the Viking!'

'Come on, girls,' Randi was saying with a note of panic in her voice. 'If you don't get your make-up on *now*, you'll be late for the photographer.'

Thank God, Jane thought, for Randi's good sense. Maybe now they'd get down to business and all she'd have to put up with was the heat and the pounding. But when she glanced over their way, she could see that even Randi, in spite of her anxiety, was goggling out of the window right along with the other two.

Just then, the blonde turned and caught Jane's eye. She shrugged in a helpless gesture and grinned broadly.

'If you can't lick 'em, join 'em,' she said tolerantly. 'You'd better come and join the crowd, Jane. I doubt if you'll get any work done today anyway. I give up.'

'I'm going to try, at least,' Jane said grouchily, and opened the folder on her desk that contained the August layout.

She'd been working hard on her own water-colours, more to fill in time than anything else, and had come up with four paintings of her favourite roses she was hoping to use in the next issue of the magazine. She'd need the managing editor's permission, though, and had made up her mind to tackle him today on the subject.

'Oh, come on, Jane,' Jennifer cried. 'You don't want to miss the show.'

'Yes, I do,' Jane replied firmly.

She glanced at her watch. Stan would be in his office now and with luck, in a good mood. He loved the heat. She took a deep breath, gathered up her paintings in the folder, and started towards the door.

Nothing ventured, nothing gained, she said to herself. All he can do is say no. When she was half-way across the room, Randi reached out and took hold of her arm.

'Jane, you've got to see this. It's a once-in-a-lifetime spectacle you'll never forget.'

'I can't, Randi,' she said brusquely, pulling away from her. 'I've got work to do even if the rest of you haven't.'

Randi's pale blue eyes widened, and she dropped her hand from Jane's arm as though she'd been burned.

'Well, sure,' she said, turning away. 'I wouldn't want to interfere with your work.'

Immediately, Jane was contrite. 'Randi,' she said, 'I'm sorry, it's the heat. It always makes me grouchy. Forgive me?'

Randi turned back to her, wavering. She was basically so good-natured that she wouldn't hold a grudge, but the hurt look was still on her face. Jane felt awful. Randi had been a good friend to her. Their working relationship had always run smoothly, Now, she'd hurt her feelings, and all because of this dratted heat.

'Come on,' she said with a smile, 'let's take a look.'

'You won't believe it,' Randi said, the hurt forgotten. 'It's like a candy store over there.'

They walked over to the window, and when she looked across the way, Jane could hardly believe

her eyes. It was like a sea of bare bodies, glistening
with sweat in the glaring sunlight. There must have
been twenty men over there, all of them working
as close to the edge of building as possible, all of
them bare-chested, and some of them with their
work trousers hanging dangerously low on near-
invisible hips.

Jane had to smile. It was indeed a veritable
candy store of male pulchritude. Short and tall,
blond, brunette, even a red-head or two, they
were all young, all at least passably good-looking,
and all rippling with well-developed muscles.

They seemed to be making token efforts at
getting their work done, but they still managed to
spend an awful lot of their time waving, calling
out wordlessly, or simply strutting around and
striking poses.

Before she even realised she was doing so, Jane
searched the group of men for a sight of Blake. He
didn't seem to be there, and she was surprised at
how disappointed this made her feel. She'd kept
her thoughts of him at bay so religiously that she'd
come to believe she'd forgotton all about him.
Apparently, she was wrong.

Annoyed at herself for even looking for him, she
moved away from the others. It was time to get on
with her visit to the managing editor about her
paintings. She'd tried to be a good sport about
admiring the view with the models, but she'd had
enough by now.

Then she saw him. He was standing over to one
side, back about twenty feet from the other men
and leaning over a set of blueprints that were
spread out on top of a long trestle table. His back
had been towards her, so she hadn't recognised
him, but now he'd turned round.

She couldn't tear her eyes away from him. It had been nearly two months since she'd even caught a glimpse of him, and she'd never seen him like this. He, too, was shirtless, wearing only a worn faded pair of jeans and heavy boots.

He stood now with his knuckles resting on his lean hips, glaring at the men clustered at the edge of the building. His upper body was glistening and tapered up from his low-slung jeans over a flat abdomen to a smooth broad chest and wide shoulders. He was deeply tanned, and his black hair was thick and shining in the sunlight.

His gaze shifted from his men to the window where the three models stood giggling. He gave them a stern, searching look, then smiled briefly and shrugged his wide shoulders in a gesture of resignation.

Then, before she could move a muscle, the dazzling blue eyes flicked her way. The smile faded instantly. She felt his narrow gaze boring into her, penetrating, questioning, almost accusing.

After what seemed like hours, an eternity, he finally turned and started walking towards the men, a set, determined look on his face. As though released by an inner spring, Jane whirled around and ran hurriedly out of the room, clutching her folder so tight in her hands that the sharp edge of it cut into her skin.

After that, from then on, she seemed to see him everywhere, and each time she did, it was like a knife turning in her heart. Then she'd have to try once more, slowly, patiently, agonisingly, to get free of her obsession with him.

She'd catch sight of him out on the streets, or gazing into a shop widow, or sitting at the counter of a restaurant. Then one night, when she was with Robert, she saw him at a concert at the Opera House. He was with Monica, and Jane assumed that meant the engagement was back on. They made a striking couple, she thought wistfully, both so tall, so tanned, so good-looking.

In the next few days, the hot spell finally broke, and Jane began to get herself back on an even keel again. After seeing Blake with Monica, she even considered agreeing to marry Robert just to put an end to her indecision about her future once and for all. He had begun making impatient noises about setting a date, and when she reminded him that they hadn't actually decided definitely to get married in the first place yet, he'd turned sullen and sulked for the rest of the evening.

She'd have to do something, she thought after that, and soon. It simply wasn't fair to keep Robert dangling. He was ready for marriage. If she removed herself from the picture, he could go on to find someone else. But was that what she wanted? She'd never vacillated like this before in her life, and she didn't like it.

The one bright spot these days was that she'd received permission from Stan, her managing editor, to use her watercolours of roses in the August edition. He'd been quite enthusiastic about them, as a matter of fact, and thought they made an interesting change from the usual photographs.

She was taking her holiday this year the last two weeks in July, and had decided to spend the time painting. The garden was pretty well under control by now, and she really didn't feel like going anywhere. With Stan's encouragement, she was anxious to get started.

On the first Saturday evening of her holiday,

then, she sat at the dining-room table at her house working on a sketch of autumn-blooming flowers. It was an intricate design, and she had just started drawing in a pencil outline on the white wash paper, when the doorbell rang.

With a sigh of irritation, she laid her pencil down and went to the door. It was still early and quite light out, so she had no qualms about slipping the chain off the hook and pulling the door wide open.

When she saw Blake standing there, looking dazzling in a well-fitting pair of chino trousers and a pale blue knit shirt that set off his tan and the colour of his eyes to perfection, her legs felt wobbly and her heart began to thud painfully.

'Hello,' he said simply.

Then he smiled. It's not fair, she said to herself, for any man to look like that. Especially one I know I can't have.

'Hello, Blake,' she said quietly, and was astounded at how calm her voice sounded.

They stood staring at each other for several seconds, neither of them saying a word, until finally Blake drew in a deep breath and expelled it slowly in a long sigh.

'Listen, Jane,' he said. 'You've got to help me out. In the past few months I've fired three landscape architects, and I'm beginning to think I may just have to pour concrete all over the place and paint it green. Maybe a little red and yellow here and there to look like flowers. Or maybe I should just use artificial turf and stick plastic blossoms around for colour.'

By this time, Jane was grinning in spite of herself. She *did* want the job, and she *had* missed him. Surely by now she would be able to withstand his appeal? So he made her heart beat a little faster. So she loved just looking at him, being with him. It didn't necessarily follow that she had to fall into his arms the minute he crooked his little finger. Perhaps they could be friends.

What would be the harm? She knew he was forever out of her reach. Did that mean she had to deny herself the pleasure of his company, his friendship? Was she so weak that she couldn't even be around him once in a while without losing her head over him?

Not sane, sensible Jane, she thought. It was a matter of pride. She owed it to herself and to him to prove that she could do it. A warm glow of self-satisfaction began to spread through her. It was going to be all right. He seemed to be safely back with Monica, anyway, and she'd probably drift into marrying Robert eventually.

'Well?' he said. 'How about it? Can I come in so we can at least discuss it?'

She opened the door a little wider. 'All right, Blake. Come on in and we'll talk about it, but . . .'

'Don't worry,' he interrupted. He held up his hands. 'Just friends.' He was inside by now, and she shut the door behind him. 'I apologise for getting out of line,' he went on in a casual tone. 'You were probably right. You were, well, different, a challenge perhaps, but I see now that a serious, practical girl like you would be miserable dealing with what I had in mind.'

She eyed him narrowly. His handsome face was the picture of innocence. 'Are you making fun of me?' she asked suspiciously.

'Heaven forbid!' he intoned piously. 'The furthest thing from my mind.' He flashed her a brilliant smile. 'Come on, Jane, trust me. I made a mistake. I admit it. Let's put it behind us and get on with the job. OK?'

He seemed sincere, she thought. It was worth a try. She didn't think he was the kind of man to pursue one woman while he was engaged to another. Besides, she knew quite well that when he said she was 'different', what he meant was that he didn't find her physically desirable anyway.

'OK,' she said at last. 'Where shall we start?'

'Well, where did we leave off? You showed me your rough sketches. You'll probably want to make more accurate measurements first.'

Her cheeks burned as she recalled that the sketches she'd made were now ashes. There was no need to tell him that, however, and blow the whole thing out of proportion.

'Right,' she agreed quickly. 'I'd better drive out to your place and do that. I'll be on vacation for the next two weeks, so the timing will be great.' It will also mean, she added to herself, that I can go out there during the week when he's at work. 'I'll drive out Monday or Tuesday and get started.'

If he was disappointed that she intended to go to his house when she knew he'd be gone, he gave no indication of it. He only nodded his head in agreement.

They were standing in the dining area now, and once again he examined the floral paintings that were hung on the wall.

'These really are quite good, you know.'

'Thank you,' she said. 'Apparently my boss agrees with you. He's going to let me use some in the next few issues.'

He glanced towards the table where she'd been working, then, and inspected the design she'd begun to sketch out.

'You ought to get a sampling together and see if you can't get a book of them out,' he mused idly. Then he looked at her. 'You're very talented.'

'Oh,' she said, a little flustered at the compliment, 'a book like that would be a very expensive proposition.'

'There are small local presses in the Puget Sound area that specialise in things like that,' he persisted. 'Wouldn't hurt to give it a try.'

'No,' she said slowly, 'I guess it wouldn't. I'll think about it.'

'You do that,' he said brusquely, then, 'I'll be on my way now. I take it we're back in business again?'

She walked with him to the front door. 'Yes,' she said. 'I'd really like to give it a try.'

'Good. Perhaps you can give me a progress report when you have something concrete to show me.'

'Yes, of course. I'll let you know.'

Then he was gone. When she'd closed the door behind him and was alone in the house once again, she felt very pleased with herself. That was an interesting idea he'd had about trying to get a collection of her paintings together and look for a publisher. But, more than that, the meeting had gone off quite well, without a trace or an undercurrent of personal feeling.

It was going to be all right, she told herself as she went back to her painting.

On Monday, she put on her oldest jeans, her sturdiest pair of shoes and a cool cotton shirt and drove out to Blake's house right after breakfast. She brought along her hundred-foot metal tape

measure, some wooden stakes for markers, a ball
of twine and a sketch pad.

When she got there, the gate of the chainlink
fence was open, as though he'd been expecting her,
and she drove through it down the winding road
to the house with an odd feeling of possessiveness.
It was, indeed, a beautiful piece of property, and
would be made even more so with the addition of
a more cultivated garden in the immediate vicinity
of the low, sprawling house.

There was no sign of life, no yellow sports car to
mar the cool greens and earth tones of the setting,
and not a trace of Blake or his car. She parked in
front of the house and got out. As she stood there
debating where to begin, she was filled with an
intense feeling of peaceful isolation, as though she
were the only human being in the universe.

To the east, the morning sun gleamed on the
peaks of the Cascade range, still lightly covered
with patches of white, the remains of the winter
snows, and all around her were the cedars, firs,
maples and birch of the forest. The air was crisp
and clear. It was going to be a fine day, perfect for
heavy work. It never got too warm at this height,
and the towering canopy of greenery tempered the
heat of the summer sun.

She could hear the gentle babbling of the creek
at the back of the house, at its lowest ebb in the
summer, but still fed by the mountain springs and
melting snow. Birds twittered noisily among the
topmost branches of the trees, busy at their
morning foraging, and in the distance she could
hear a woodpecker tapping away.

There were golden eagles' nests up here, she
thought, as she walked around the house to the
creek at the back. Perhaps she'd see one today.

They were often visible, even in the city, soaring high above the bustle and noise.

She had decided to start with the back of the house, not only because the rushing creek offered a lovely focal point, but because Blake obviously spent a lot of time out there on the partially covered veranda entertaining. It was where he'd served her dinner that evening in May, the first time she'd been out here.

Glancing up at the veranda now, she couldn't help remembering that evening they'd sat out there in the gathering dusk, chatting, getting acquainted, talking about their work, the garden project. She'd felt so comfortable with him then, so at ease, and she had the feeling he enjoyed her company as much as she did his.

Then later, she thought, when he'd taken her home, suddenly everything had changed. She'd fallen off the stool and he'd caught her, and she had found herself thrust into a totally new dimension. She could still recall, with a gentle insistent throbbing of her pulses, the way she'd felt in his arms, the hand on her breast, the fine mouth pressing on hers, warm and moist and intimate.

'Stop it!' she said aloud. With a little shake of her head, she made herself tear her eyes away from the veranda that had aroused those memories. She marched purposefully back to her car, got out her stakes and string and tape measure, and prepared to set to work.

She laboured steadily for three hours, totally absorbed in the task at hand. At the end of that time she was hot, dusty and exhausted. She was also very hungry, she realised, as she walked slowly around examining her morning's work. Next time I'll bring along a lunch, she decided.

She'd accomplished a great deal that morning, but it was becoming clear that the job was going to be far more extensive than she'd first imagined. There was simply an awful lot of ground to be covered. She'd have to spend her whole holiday out here to do it right.

At least she had a pretty accurate sketch now of the area immediately surrounding the house. She could do a lot of the actual detail planning at home. Still, she wanted to get each section staked out on the terrain itself to make it easier when it came time to plant. They'd have to wait until autumn for that, but in the meantime the construction of paths and the preparation of the beds could begin.

While she'd been staking and measuring, she'd spotted and listed several varieties of native plants she could use: Oregon grape, salal, sumac, kinnickinick, wild huckleberry, trillium and vine maple. Some of these weren't easily domesticated, but with luck the lavish use of natives would blend nicely with the shrubs she needed to purchase.

As she drove home, still mentally concentrated on the project, she suddenly realised how happy she'd been all morning, in spite of the tiring, sweaty work. She began to understand why Blake loved his own job. There was a lot of satisfaction in physical labour, she thought. No wonder he didn't want to give it up, not even for the lovely Monica.

However, she recalled with a little twinge of regret, that situation seemed to have resolved itself, and she wondered who had given in. Somehow, she didn't think it had been Blake.

Jane continued to go out to Blake's every morning

for the next week. She took lunch with her now, and would continue on after she ate until three o'clock, the time when she knew Blake would be leaving work and coming home. She still was convinced it would be better all round if they didn't meet. Besides, she was worn out by then and ready to leave.

At the weekend it rained, a typical phenomenon in Seattle, virtually the one aspect of its capricious weather pattern you could count on. It was just as well, Jane thought, as she settled down to her own painting at the dining-table after breakfast on Saturday. She'd been neglecting her work, and now she wouldn't even be tempted to drive out to Blake's in the rain.

She was a little concerned about the progress report she had promised him. Several times during the week she had considered calling him, but she always changed her mind at the last minute. The work she'd done would be obvious to him anyway, since the place was rapidly sprouting stakes and string in every conceivable potential garden space. No need to call him just yet. And he hadn't called her, so he couldn't be concerned.

She had kept meticulous records of her time and expenses. They hadn't discussed whether he would want her to supervise the actual construction and planting, and her intention was to present him with a detailed, itemised bill on the day she handed him the completed plans. They could negotiate then about any supervision he wanted her to do.

Keeping track of her time and the money she expended on petrol and supplies helped her keep the whole venture on an impersonal, businesslike plane. She still felt a little guilty about charging him for work she enjoyed to much, but, aside from the fact that she knew he was well able to afford it, it was absolutely necessary to her own peace of mind to view Blake Bannister exclusively as her employer.

By Monday morning, of course, the heavy grey sky had broken up into fluffy white clouds, and the sun appeared once again in a blue sky. Looking out of her kitchen window at the sunlight glistening on the remaining raindrops in the garden, Jane smiled to herself as she recalled the old Seattle joke about the man who was late for work one Monday morning because it had been raining when he woke up. He'd simply turned over and gone back to sleep, assuming that it was still the weekend.

Jane gathered her belongings and got into her car to drive out to Blake's. She had five more days of holiday to work on it, and she was so anxious to get at it that she skipped breakfast. She could drive into Fall City around eleven for a meal.

When she got there, the gate was open as usual, and she drove down the road with her head full of plans for her day's work. She'd finished with the areas adjacent to the house and was going to start today with the outlying gardens that merged into the surrounding woods.

As she drove, she kept one eye on the now-familiar road, the other on the terrain, considering the possibilities in each section, so that she had stopped the car in front of the house before she realised that he must be home.

She saw his car first, parked in the open garage, and at the sight of it her heart began to race erratically. While she was still trying to assimilate the significance of that fact, she looked up to see him strolling down the steps of the house towards her. She could only stare at him, speechless, her heart pounding, her hands stuck clammily to the steering wheel, watching him come nearer and nearer to her.

When he got to the car, he braced his hands on the roof and leaned over to look in at her through the open window. It had only been a week since she'd seen him, but every time with him was like the first time. The sight of him simply left her breathless, and she fought hard now to get herself back under control.

'Good morning,' he said with a wide, friendly smile. 'Have you had breakfast?'

'No,' she stammered without thinking. Then she gave him a sharp look. 'What are you doing here?'

He opened the car door and stepped back to let her out. 'I live here,' he said drily, 'remember?'

She got out of the car and stood facing him. He was dressed in worn but clean blue jeans and a white knit shirt. He looked as though he'd just stepped out of the shower and had recently shaved. In the clear morning air, the scent of soap wafted her way, and when he turned his head to shut the car door, she could see that the dark thick hair at the back of his neck was still a little damp.

'You know what I mean,' she said. 'Why aren't you at work?'

'There's another strike. Electricians this time.' He started walking towards the garage. When she only stood there staring after his tall, lean-hipped figure, he turned round. 'Come on,' he urged. 'I'm going to take you out for breakfast.'

Oh, well, she thought, what harm could one breakfast do? It was broad daylight, after all. Besides, she was glad to see him, and there were things they had to discuss about the project. Not only that, she recalled, as she slowly walked towards him, he was safely engaged again to Monica.

'Have you ever been to Snoqualmie Falls Lodge?' he asked as they got inside his car.

'No, I haven't,' she said. She was feeling more at ease with him now. There was nothing about him in the least threatening. It was all in her own mind. She turned to him with a little laugh. 'I've heard about it all my life, of course, but somehow never got around to going there. I've never been through the Ballard Locks, either.'

'Well, I hope you're hungry,' he said as he started the engine. 'They put on a terrific spread for breakfast.'

He laid his arm along the back of the seat and turned his head around to see behind him as he backed out of the garage, bringing his face much nearer to hers. She gazed stonily straight ahead until he had turned the car around and they were moving forward.

'I've been wanting to have a talk with you,' he said as he drove. 'But you're always gone by the time I get home. From all the little stakes and string you've put up all over the place, it looks as though you've been busy.'

'I start quite early,' she said, glancing at him a little defensively. 'I've kept track of my time very accurately.'

'I'm sure you have. I knew I could count on you to do the efficient, practical thing.' The blue gaze flicked briefly at her. 'You called it your one great virtue, as I recall.'

She didn't know what to reply to that, and they drove on in silence through the little village of Fall City and up higher into the mountains on the narrow winding road that ran alongside the river. When they came to the Lodge, Jane drew in her breath sharply at the sheer beauty of the setting.

To the right of the low, rather small structure that housed the restaurant, and much higher up, the falls poured over the cliff in a roaring torrent, foaming down into the river below. It was a spectacular sight, even in July, when the water was at its lowest volume. At the edge of the deep ravine below the falls was a narrow concrete path with a chainlink guard-rail alongside it where visitors could view the falls at a closer level.

'After breakfast we can go take a look if you'd like,' Blake said as he parked the car in the small paved lot in front of the Lodge.

When they got outside, the roaring of the water was deafening, and the spray of it filled the air. The parking lot was full, since summer was their busiest season with the influx of tourists into the area. Jane wondered if they'd have trouble being seated, but when they went up the steps and got inside, Blake marched confidently up to the hostess at the cash register.

'Bannister,' he said clearly. 'I made reservations for two at ten o'clock.'

Jane stood there staring at him. Reservations?

CHAPTER SEVEN

JANE watched, stunned, as the cheerful young waitress started serving them the Lodge's standard breakfast almost as soon as they were seated. They had a table by the window overlooking the falls, and even through the double pane of glass, the roar of that mighty torrent was still audible.

They started with coffee and freshly squeezed orange juice, followed by a large plate of fresh fruit: several kinds of melon, pineapple, strawberries and blueberries. Then came steaming bowls of porridge, cooked the old-fashioned way and left to simmer all night long. With it was a pitcher of heavy cream and a bowl of brown sugar.

It wasn't until they were served their eggs, cooked to order, that Jane's stomach began to rebel, and when the smiling waitress held a spoonful of golden honey high in the air to let it drip slowly down on to the freshly made waffles, already smothered in butter, she gave Blake a look of dismay.

The waitress set down a plate filled with sausage, bacon and ham slices, poured fresh cups of coffee, then departed, telling them she'd be back later to see if they needed anything more and hoping they'd enjoy their breakfast.

'Blake,' Jane whispered, leaning across the table, 'I can't possibly eat all this.'

He was already tucking in with gusto, just as though he hadn't already consumed a bowl of porridge, three-quarters of the fruit plate and three waffles. Where did he put it all? She wondered, glancing at the trim athletic body.

He gestured in the air with his fork and swallowed what he'd been chewing. 'No problem. Eat what you can. It helps to take a break now and then. There's no hurry.'

He reached across the table and covered her plate with the round metal lid to keep it warm, then went back to shovelling in more scrambled egg and sausage.

Jane sat back in her chair with a groan. She'd just noticed the pile of pancakes behind her omelette before Blake had covered the plate. 'I won't be able to eat again for a week! It's all so delicious, too. I hate to waste any of it.'

'Not sorry you came, then?' he asked between bites.

'Oh, no. It's a wonderful place.' Then she remembered. 'But I'm curious about one thing.'

He raised his eyebrows. 'What's that?'

She put her elbows on the table and eyed him narrowly. 'The reservations. You were pretty sure of yourself, weren't you? What if I'd already had breakfast and decided not to come?'

He shrugged and pushed his empty plate away from him. 'You did, didn't you?'

'That's no answer,' she said, exasperated.

He lit a cigarette and inhaled deeply, then settled back in his chair with a sigh of contentment and smiled at her. 'I would have cancelled the reservation. Or come alone.'

'You've got an answer for everything, haven't you?' she said with grudging admiration. Really, she thought, it was hard to stay annoyed with him when he sat there looking like that.

He lifted his chin and blew out one perfect

smoke ring, then shrugged again. 'I try to.' The blue eyes flashed at her from beneath half-closed lids. 'Consider it a business breakfast. Tell me how far you've progressed with your plans.'

As she explained what she intended to do with the garden, she idly removed the cover from her dish and started picking at the still-warm omelette. Before she realised what she was doing, she had finished it, plus another waffle, plus two slices of Canadian bacon.

When she was through, she looked down at her empty plate with astonishment. 'I can't believe I did that,' she said. 'I am totally absolutely stuffed.'

Blake laughed and scraped his chair back. 'I think we could both use some exercise.' He stood up and looked down at her. 'Let's go see the falls.'

After he paid the bill, they walked outside into the sunshine and started up the narrow path that led to the falls. As they came closer, the spray in the air became heavier, until Jane could feel its cool touch on her face and hair. There were several other people on the path, most of them looking like tourists with children in tow and cameras slung around their necks.

At the top of the path, the roar was deafening. They stood leaning over the fence, watching the torrential cascade of water pouring over the edge and down into the deep chasm several hundred feet below where it rushed, foaming, into the river.

Blake leaned over to speak close to her ear. 'Quite a sight, isn't it?'

She turned to him and smiled. 'It's perfectly magnificent!'

Their eyes met and held for a long moment. Jane's smile faded gradually as she became intensely aware once again of the power this man had over her. Her eyes widened with a slight jab of panic, but then, as though sensing it, he casually turned away and gazed fixedly at the falls.

It occurred to her then that he knew exactly what was going on in her mind, was well aware of his power over her, but, for some reason, had decided not to take advantage of it. She sensed vaguely that she could trust him not to use her weakness where he was concerned for his own ends, and her panic began to ebb away.

As she relaxed, however, she had to wonder why he was sticking so resolutely to his agreement to keep their relationship on a friendly impersonal basis. She saw now that she had been foolish to imagine she had anything to fear from him on that score. And, perhaps, she had to admit, a little vain. He was keeping his promise for the simple reason that he wasn't physically attracted to her.

The one time in their whole acquaintance that he had approached her physically in any way, that night in her kitchen, had been due to their propinquity and, as he himself admitted, the fact that she was different from the other women he had known. Plain Janes were something new to his experience, an oddity, and, of course, being the kind of completely self-assured man he was, a challenge.

Added to that was the fact that he had just broken his engagement to Monica Mason. He was on the rebound, and she was the first woman to quite literally fall into his arms after that. He must have cared deeply about Monica, Jane thought as they walked slowly back down the path to the car, to have been so hurt.

Now they were back together again, Monica and Blake, probably re-engaged. She wanted very much to ask him on the way back to his place if they were, but then she thought, what difference does it make? Whatever their status, they obviously belonged together, and that was that.

So, she said to herself as they drove along in silence, I have absolutely nothing to worry about, and I'm grateful. Now we can work together, even be friends. I'm really very happy it turned out this way.

But when they got back to the house and he left her immediately, telling her he knew she was anxious to get back on the job and that he had work of his own to do in the house, why was it that, watching him walk away from her towards the house, she didn't feel very happy?

Once she got started with her stakes and tape measure again, however, the mood passed, and she became totally absorbed in the work at hand. Most likely, she decided, the slight depression had been due more to the enormous breakfast than any lingering attraction she might feel for Blake.

By three o'clock, she was ready to leave and go home. She hadn't seen a sign of Blake since they got back from the Lodge that morning, and she assumed he must have had a lot of paperwork to catch up on during the electricians' strike.

She gathered her things together and was putting them in the back seat of the car when he appeared at the front porch.

'Quitting time?' he called to her.

'I think so,' she said, turning to face him. 'Actually, I've gone as far as I can here on the site. I won't charge you for my time at breakfast,' she went on with a smile, 'since you paid for it.'

'Now, that's what I call a fair-minded attitude,' he said, walking towards her. 'I wish my men were so generous.' He was beside her now, near the car. 'What's the next step?' he asked.

'I hope to have a detailed set of plans for you in about a week, but I can work on those at home. When I finish, I'll have them blueprinted for you and give you a set. There's a good graphics lab across the street from the office, and they've done work for me in the past.'

'OK,' he said. 'Then what? When do I get my garden?'

She looked at him. 'I've been meaning to speak to you about that,' she said slowly. 'There are three stages in building a garden.' She ticked them off on her fingers. 'The planning, which I hope to complete next week. Then the construction and preparation of beds, which you'll have to hire out or get your crew out here to work on. Then the last step is the actual planting, and that will have to wait until, say, November.'

'November!' he exclaimed. 'Why so long?'

'Well, the preparation and construction take time,' she explained. 'But most of all, you can't just yank growing things out of the ground and stick them in somewhere else any old time. Plants have definite cycles of growth and rest. You move them when they're resting and leave them alone when they're growing.'

He looked so disappointed, just like a little boy who has been told he can't have the train set he longs for until Christmas, that she had trouble keeping a straight face. Yet even in her amusement at his chagrin, her heart went out to him. No matter what this man was thinking or doing or feeling, she thought, he was so appealing it made her ache in every fibre of her being.

'A garden requires patience,' she said gently.

'Like all good things in this world, you have to give it a chance to become what it's meant to be. It's futile and destructive to force it.'

The expression on his face was gradually transformed from one of almost petulant disappointment to a dawning look of frank admiration.

'For someone so young,' he said slowly, 'you've accumulated a lot of wisdom. Your Robert's a lucky guy.' He gave a self-deprecating laugh. 'All right,' he said, 'I'll be patient if it kills me, although, unlike you, Miss Fairchild, it's not one of my virtues.'

'All the more reason to cultivate it, then,' she said drily.

'Tell me, then, O wise one,' he said, 'what are your weaknesses?'

You are, was the thought that popped immediately into her head, but she dismissed it instantly and smiled coolly at him.

'Believe me, you wouldn't be interested. They're very dull.'

She turned and got inside the car, but before she had a chance to start it, he leaned his head down and spoke to her through the window.

'You *are* going to follow through on this whole thing for me, aren't you?' he asked.

'You mean supervise the construction and planting?'

'Well, someone's got to do it, and I sure as hell wouldn't even know where to start.'

'I don't know, Blake,' she said slowly. 'It will take an awful lot of time. Let me think about it. If I decide I can't do it, I know several good people who can.'

He thought for a moment. 'That's fair enough,'

he said. He straightened up. 'I'll expect to hear
from you, then, when the plans are finished.'

'Right,' she said. She fired the engine and
started backing the car around. 'Goodbye, then.
Thanks for the breakfast.'

He only nodded, and her last view of him, as she
turned to drive off, was standing there alone,
looking straight and tall and magnificent against
the background of green forest and blue sky, his
dark head lifted slightly, his hands tucked into the
back pockets of his jeans.

By the time Jane returned to work the following
Monday, she had finished the plans for Blake's
garden and the watercolour she intended to use for
the September issue of the magazine.

A very profitable holiday, she thought, as she
walked across the street on her lunch hour to have
Blake's plans blueprinted. She had also completed
a full statement to present to him for her time and
expenses so far. She still hadn't made up her mind
about going on with the supervision of the actual
work, but there was plenty of time for that. First
they'd have to go over the plans together and
make any necessary changes.

That night when she got home from work, she
decided to call him to let him know the plans were
ready and to set up an appointment for a meeting
to discuss them. She had just slipped off her shoes,
removed her stockings and padded into the hall
where she kept the telephone, when it started to ring.

'Jane? It's Blake,' he said when she answered it.

As usual, the sound of his voice made her heart
flop over and a tingling sensation run up and
down her spine. She admonished herself sternly to
stop that nonsense and put on her most

businesslike tone of voice.

'I was just now going to call you,' she said. 'The plans are all finished.'

'Good,' he said with satisfaction. 'See how patient I've been? I haven't pestered you about them for a whole week.'

She had the insane urge to tell him he'd been a good boy, but stifled the impulse. If he'd been there, she thought wryly, she would have patted him on the head. That wonderful dark head, she added, with a little inward sigh.

'You see,' she said instead, 'it does come with practice.'

'I'll be right over,' he said.

So much for patience, she thought. 'Now?'

'Sure. Why not?'

Because I might have made other plans, she said to herself a little crossly. Then she thought, well, why not? She *didn't* have other plans, after all, and they did have to discuss it.

'Shall I bring Chinese food?' he was going on without waiting for a reply. 'Or would you rather go out?'

She quickly searched her mind for what she might have on hand. There was fresh crab her fisherman neighbour had given her yesterday. She could hard boil some eggs, and there were tomatoes and lettuce in the garden, rolls in the freezer.

'I'll fix us something,' she said. 'How does Crab Louis sound?'

'You ask a Seattle native such a question? Give me a half-hour. No, twenty-minutes.'

'Hold on,' she said laughing. 'You've been home since three. I just got off work. Make it an hour.'

*   *   *

That night after dinner, they sat at the dining-room table going over the plans in great detail. She had made a coloured ink drawing of what she envisaged the finished product would look like, giving the overall picture, including the house itself and the surrounding native woodlands.

He listened intently, asked one or two questions to clarify a few points, and when they had finished, he leaned back in his chair and gave her a long satisfied look.

'I'm impressed,' he said slowly. 'It's exactly what I hoped for.'

'Now, it's not going to happen overnight,' she warned him. 'It's got to progress in slow stages, but I think by next spring, it should at least come close to this.' She held up the drawing.

He took it from her and gazed at it for a long time. 'You've made it come to life,' he said at last. He started rolling up his set of blueprints. 'These are mine?' he asked.

'Yes.' She was just about to offer a cup of coffee or a drink, when he got up from his chair.

'Well, I'll be on my way, then. Thanks for dinner.'

Feeling a little crushed at his abrupt withdrawal, she slowly rose to her feet and followed him to the front door. When they got there, he turned to her.

'Have you come to a decision about going on with the project?'

She hadn't, but now that the plans were actually completed, she knew it was time to make up her mind. Still, she hesitated. Everything in her wanted to do it, as much for the pleasure of prolonging her relationship with Blake, she had to admit, as it was for the satisfaction of seeing it through to the end.

That's what worried her, however. The more she was around him, the more she came to like him. Was that foolish? Even dangerous? She looked up at him. He was obviously impatient to leave. She wouldn't have to worry about any overtures from him, at any rate, so what was her problem? Since he was so patently uninterested in her, there would be no temptation to succumb to.

'Yes,' she said finally, 'I'd like to do it.'

'Good,' he said, pulling the door open. 'It looks as though the Houston project is going to go ahead, so I'll be gone a lot this fall and winter anyway and won't get in your way or bother you with my impatient questions.'

With that, he was out the door and gone.

At this stage of the proceedings, all Jane really had to do was get the men started on the construction and digging, then drive out to Blake's every few days to inspect it and make sure they were following her instructions. It was the middle of August now, and the days were quite long, giving her lots of time after work to make fairly regular inspections.

She rarely saw Blake. True to his word, he supplied the men and equipment as she required them, but never got underfoot himself. Once or twice she saw him on the porch of the house chatting with one of the men, and they would wave and smile, but that was the only communication they had.

And I was worried about being in constant close contact with him, she mused wryly as she drove home from his place early one evening. The work had been going on for three weeks. She'd only seen him four times, at most, and hadn't spoken to him once.

The night she'd presented him with the plans, she had also enclosed her bill for services and expenses up to that point. Two days later, she'd received an official-looking letter with the Bannister Construction Company letterhead, enclosing a cheque for the full amount and a short formal letter, obviously dictated to a secretary and neatly typed, expressing his appreciation for a job well done.

Then there was Robert, she thought as she let herself in the door of her house. What in the world was she going to do about Robert? Thank goodness he was out of town again, in hot pursuit of yet more witnesses for his anti-trust case. But he'd be back in a few weeks, and she really had to have an answer for him then.

She went into the bathroom, peeled off her sticky clothes and got under the shower. One way of looking at it, she thought as she soaped herself, was that marrying Robert would put her out of the way of temptation with Blake. Then she snorted. What temptation? He treated her as he would one of his workmen!

She rinsed off, stepped out on to the bath mat and started drying off. On the other hand, she thought, marrying Robert would mean she'd be *married* to Robert! Was that what she wanted? No! The answer came from the deepest, truest depths of her being. Even if, as she suspected, the real reason was that every man paled in comparison with Blake Bannister, she still didn't want to spend the rest of her life as Robert's wife.

With that issue settled firmly in her mind at last, she felt a distinct lightening of her spirits. She'd been feeling very guilty about Robert. Now, as soon as he got back, she'd tell him. She hoped they could remain friends, but if not, she'd just have to live with it. It certainly was not possible to continue on as they had been.

The telephone rang just then. Wrapping herself in the towel, she went into the hall to answer it.

'Hello.'

'Do you like chamber music?'

The sound of Blake's voice played its familiar trick on her, and she sank slowly into the nearby chair.

'Yes,' she said, 'very much.'

'Good. I have two tickets for the Guarneri concert tonight at Meany Hall. I'll pick you up in half an hour and we can grab a bite to eat on the way.'

She didn't know what to say. The way he barged in and out of her life simply made her head spin. She hadn't spoken to him, had hardly even seen him, for three weeks, and now here he was, expecting her to drop everything and go out with him at a moment's notice. He was an insufferable, arrogant, high-handed . . .

But, on the other hand, she wanted to go. She asked herself what she would have done if it had been Robert calling at the last minute like that, and the answer was simple. She would have done exactly what she felt like doing. What was the difference with Blake? They were only friends.

'All right,' she said at last. 'Half an hour.'

So what, she said to herself as she got dressed, if at the last minute Monica couldn't go and he'd called her as a last resort. It wouldn't have bothered her in the slightest if Robert had done so. If the sensible thing was to treat Blake as only a friend, then the sensible thing was to take advantage of an opportunity to go to a concert she genuinely wanted to hear.

Half an hour later, on the dot, Jane was ready. Her thick hair was cut in a style that only required washing and blow-drying. She wore no make-up except for a little lipstick. And there was never any agonising indecision over what to wear, since her whole wardrobe consisted of practically identical outfits that varied only in colour and weight with the seasons.

Her only hesitation was over her lingerie, and she picked through the carefully folded garments until she came to the filmiest, laciest white bra and half-slip she owned. It doesn't really make any difference what I wear on the outside, she thought as she slipped them on over her bare skin, when I know what's on underneath.

She did, however, choose what she considered her most flattering outfit, an oyster linen tailored dress with a matching jacket. She'd been out in the sun so much lately that her skin was nicely tanned, and her hair—the colour of ripe chestnuts, Blake had once said—gleamed against the pale suit.

Not glamorous or provocative, she thought as she surveyed her reflection in the mirror, but not exactly a dowdy frump, either. Since her taste in clothes was so simple, she bought good ones meant to last. Not only that, she mused with a secret smile, but the daring lingerie she wore made her feel sexy and desirable even though no one would ever see it.

They decided to have a light supper before the concert at a little Czech restaurant in Pioneer

Square. It was on the way, and the service would be prompt on a weekday night. Jane had been there before and was very fond of their speciality, a fruit plate with different kinds of sausage and small individual loaves of freshly-baked rye bread.

As they walked together from Blake's car to the restaurant, Jane couldn't help recalling the first night she'd met him, back in March on the night of Fat Tuesday. In fact, they were on the very same street, but tonight, five months later, the sun was still shining at six-thirty, while that night it had been dark and raining.

Blake, as always, looked gorgeous in a lightweight navy blue blazer, grey trousers and a crisp white shirt. She'd never seen him in a tie before, and it occurred to her that he looked just as much at home in formal wear as he did in his rough work clothes. She also noticed, as they walked down the street and then, later, to their table inside the restaurant, that more than one appreciative female glance was cast his way.

Remember, she warned herself sternly when they were seated across from each other, he's only a friend. Hardly even that. He's my employer. Like the breakfast at Snoqualmie Falls Lodge, consider this a business meeting. She put on her most businesslike air and made herself look into those dazzling blue eyes without blinking.

'What do you think about your new garden so far?' she asked.

'I don't think much of anything yet,' he replied. 'To me it looks a lot like the excavation for a new building.' He waved a hand in the air. 'All the ditches and large holes.'

She laughed and took a sip of the wine Blake had ordered. 'Well, you should feel right at home, then. Be patient. By next April you won't recognise the place.'

'I'll take your word for that,' he said drily. Then he smiled. 'You remind me of how I had to reassure some of my early customers. I started out by building houses, you know, and only gradually progressed to skyscrapers.'

'No,' she said, somewhat surprised. 'I didn't know that. I guess I just assumed it was a family business.'

He threw back his head and laughed. 'Good God, no!' he said. 'My father was a very successful stockbroker. He fought tooth and nail against my involvement with what he called "manual labour". He did, however, leave me and my brothers each a tidy sum when he died. Enough, anyway, to get my own company going and get out of the residential field.'

'You didn't like building houses?'

He shrugged. 'I got bored with it. I had my mind set on bigger things.'

'How many brothers do you have?' she asked.

He grinned. 'Just two.'

'I envy you. I always wanted a brother or sister. Do they live here in Seattle?'

'No. Greg is a mining engineer, now living in Arabia, and Scott is an officer in the Navy. Flies jets. He's one of the Blue Angels.'

'You're a daring trio, aren't you?' she asked with a smile. 'And not one of you followed in your poor father's footsteps. Did that make him very unhappy?'

He thought this over gravely for a moment while the waitress set their dinner plates down before them.

'Yes,' he said when she had gone, 'I think it

bothered both my mother and father for a long time. But, thank God, before they died they both became reconciled to the fact that none of their sons was cut out to sit behind a desk and spend their lives pushing around pieces of paper.'

'How did they die?' she asked softly.

'Drowned,' he said brusquely, and attacked his food. 'They got caught in a storm on their boat up in the Straits of Juan de Fuca.'

'And that's why you dislike boats?'

He raised one eyebrow and gave her an appreciative glance. 'You remembered that.' He nodded. 'Yes, that's one reason, I guess. They also take too much time and attention. I'd rather be working, building things.'

They finished their light meal in less than an hour, which gave them plenty of time to get to the concert by eight. While Blake paid the bill at the cash till in front, Jane wandered around inspecting the gaily dressed dolls and lacy handmade place mats that were on display over to one side. Then, just as he came walking towards her, the door to the restaurant opened, and Randi Tatum walked in, her judge in tow.

By then, Blake had reached her side and was holding her lightly by the elbow. Randi just stood there and stared at them, the door half-open, the poor judge still standing out on the pavement. Jane almost had to laugh at the look on Randi's face as her glance flicked from Jane to Blake and then back to Jane again.

'Uh, hello, Randi,' she finally said. 'What a surprise.'

The tall blonde's eyes narrowed and she came closer, allowing her escort to get inside at last. 'Yes,' she said. 'Isn't it?'

'Do you know Blake Bannister?' Jane asked,
gesturing towards the tall man at her side.

'I believe we've met,' Randi murmured shooting
him a look that could only be described as coy,
Jane thought with disgust. Does every woman in
the world, she wondered, turn to jelly at the sight
of him?

'Well, it was nice seeing you, Randi,' Jane
murmured weakly as she started to move past her.
'We've got to be on our way.'

As they went out the door, Jane heard Blake
greet the judge by his first name, as though they
were old friends. Of course, she thought, safely out
on the pavement at last. He knows everybody. She
could still feel Randi's gimlet eyes burning into her
as they went down the street away from the
restaurant, and she knew she'd have some
explaining to do tomorrow.

Later that evening, sitting next to him at the
concert, Jane was very much aware of his intense
absorption in the music, an all-Schubert pro-
gramme. What a complex man, she thought to
herself. He loved the rough construction work he'd
been so successful at, yet had a fine appreciation
of art, music, nature. He travelled in Seattle's
highest social circles, yet had taken the time to
bring her Chinese food when she'd had her tooth
pulled out, and although on the job he had the air
of command that made him quite definitely the
boss, he also enjoyed a casual camaraderie with his
men. He seemed to have been devoted to his
parents and the close family life with them and his
two brothers, yet had decided not to marry or
have a family of his own.

Unless, she amended, the engagement with

Monica really was back on. He never talked about her, and Jane wondered if he would have asked her out tonight if he was firmly committed to another woman. Then she reminded herself that this wasn't really a date. She was still plain Jane, after all, and posed no threat to his relationship with Monica.

He might as well have asked one of his electricians, she thought, after he'd taken her home and she was getting ready for bed. He'd walked her politely to the front door, made sure she got inside safely and there were no burglars lurking in the shadows, then said good night and left.

'That's good,' she said aloud as she got into bed and switched off the light. That's exactly the way I want it, she added to herself. He wanted to go to the concert, he didn't want to waste his extra ticket, and she had enjoyed herself.

CHAPTER EIGHT

'ALL right,' Randi said the next day when they were alone in the office. 'Let's have it.'

Jane gazed up from the layout spread on the top of her desk with innocent eyes. She'd been expecting Randi to challenge her about seeing her with Blake last night ever since she'd got to work that morning, and was only grateful she'd waited until Stephanie and Jennifer were gone.

'What?' she asked, her eyes blank.

'Come on, Jane. Don't pull that act with me. I know you too well.' She was standing before her, arms akimbo and hands firmly planted on her hips. 'You and Blake Bannister, that's what.' She shook her head admiringly. 'You are a deep one, that's for sure.'

'Now listen, Randi,' Jane put in hastily, 'don't get the wrong idea. It's not like that. I'm doing a job for him, that's all, a paid job. He hired me to plan a garden for him.'

'I see,' Randi said, clearly not seeing at all. 'And just how did all this come about? I didn't even know you knew him.'

'It's a long story,' Jane said feebly. 'We just kind of ran into each other a couple of times and he found out I knew something about gardens. He has a house out in Fall City and wanted to put in a rather extensive garden. Honestly, that's all there is to it.'

'I don't believe it,' Randi said flatly. 'If there's one thing I know a little something about, it's men, and the look on his face when he came up behind you at the restaurant last night spoke volumes.'

Jane gave her a blank, uncomprehending stare. 'Randi,' she said slowly, 'I honestly don't know what you're talking about. We're just friends. I only work for him.'

Randi was slowly shaking her head from side to side. 'You know, Jane, I believe you.' She laughed shortly. 'Isn't that just like you? Nice practical, sensible Jane, happy as a clam playing in her garden and painting her pretty pictures, and then she walks off with the most eligible man in town. I've got to hand it to you, kiddo.'

'No,' Jane protested, 'you've got it all wrong, Randi.'

Just then Jennifer and Stephanie breezed into the room chattering about the bargains they'd seen that day at every store in town, and, to Jane's intense relief, Randi turned and walked off. But not without one last backward look that told Jane clearly she hadn't heard the last of the subject.

In the days that followed, it seemed that she was suddenly seeing an awful lot of Blake, but it all happened so gradually that it began to seem quite natural for him to call every other night or so to ask her if she would like to go to a concert or a film. She never saw him at his place when she went out there to check on the progress of the work, however. He always stayed out of sight then.

After a while of this, she began to feel much more at ease around him. She still found him very attractive, but by now had schooled herself not to see him in any other light except as a friend. In fact, her relationship with Blake had come to seem almost an exact duplicate of the one she'd had with Robert for so long.

Although he would take her arm on occasion when they crossed a street, or lean his head close to hers in a darkened theatre to make a comment, he always left her at the door when he took her home and never asked to come in. Their conversations were free and easy now, but not in any way flirtatious or provocative.

She was very grateful for this turn of events, she told herself many times whenever the little inner voice would whisper to her that she wanted more. She was sensible, practical Jane, and it was working out exactly as she'd hoped it would. They were friends. No emotional involvement, no hint of romance, and she finally convinced herself that it was probably her fate never to experience the transports of passion she heard discussed so endlessly by the three models.

When Robert came back from his trip, she told him one night very firmly that she didn't want to get married. She could tell the minute he walked in the house that he was all primed for a showdown, and she decided to get it over immediately.

'It's not you, Robert,' she assured him hurriedly when she saw the crestfallen look on his face. 'I just don't want to get married at all. You'll find someone else. You're a great catch, you know.'

This seemed to mollify his bruised ego a little, but she could tell he was genuinely disappointed. 'I just always took it for granted,' he said as he was leaving, 'that we'd end up together.'

'We'll always be friends,' she said, kissing him lightly on the cheek. She laughed. 'I'll be the spinster Aunt Jane to your children one day. You'll see.'

When he was gone, however, a wave of depression hit her. What a fate! Aunt Jane to other women's children! One day soon, she supposed as she walked slowly out into the garden, Blake would marrry Monica, and she'd have to sit by and watch their family, too, always on the outside looking in.

What's wrong with me? she agonised to herself. Why can't I feel what other women feel? Then she remembered the night in her kitchen when she'd almost fallen off the stool and Blake had caught her.

I certainly felt something then, she thought. Yes, she added bitterly, and was terrified out of my wits by it. Had she been wrong not to follow her heart, to let herself be carried away by those feelings Blake had aroused in her? What would have happened if she had?

She knew quite well. A short affair, certain heartbreak for her when it was over. Gradually, sanity returned, and with it came calm. Everything in her rebelled against such a course. It couldn't possibly be worth it. It was too late anyway. I'm stuck with myself the way I am, she thought with a sigh. I have my work, my home, and that will just have to be enough.

By now, the construction work on Blake's garden was almost finished. The brick paths were laid out, the beds dug in with peat moss and dried manure, and all that was left was to let the ground settle for a month or two under the autumn rains. Then, in November, the actual planting could begin.

The next day, she decided she'd better make one more trip out there, probably her last for two or three months or so. The men and equipment were

only scheduled for two more days, and she needed
to check on their progress one last time and give
them their final instructions.

The day was warm, but slightly overcast.
August was the month for morning fogs in Seattle,
and in the city, at least, it had hung on through the
afternoon, obscuring the sun and creating a muggy
atmosphere that was oppressive.

The closer she came to the mountains, however,
the clearer the air became, and by the time she
reached the turning off the main highway that led
to Blake's property, the sky had turned a pale blue
and the mist had virtually evaporated.

She'd left the office early to be sure to catch the
foreman before four o'clock, when he left for the
day. As she drove down the winding road towards
the house, she thought suddenly about her
conversation with Randi two weeks ago. It still
bothered her a little that her friend had got the
wrong impression from seeing her with Blake at
the restaurant the night before, but she had been
so busy lately she hadn't found an opportunity to
talk to her in private. She needed to explain to her
that she and Blake had a strictly impersonal
relationship before Randi got too carried away
with her romantic flights of fancy.

It puzzled Jane just a little why she would even
think a man like Blake would be interested in her
in that way in the first place, given her decidedly
unglamorous persona and Blake's reputation with
women. If it had been Stephanie or Jennifer, she
could understand it, but not plain Jane.

The foreman was still there waiting for her, and
after she'd parked her car, the two of them took a
tour of the areas under construction to make sure
they could finish up tomorrow. It did look like a

mess, Jane thought as she examined each site, just as Blake had said. But as she checked the various paths and beds with the set of plans she carried, she knew it would turn out exactly as she had envisaged it once the plantings were in.

When she was satisfied that the foreman understood what had to be done tomorrow and that he would be able to finish his work on time, they said goodbye and she watched him drive off in his pick-up truck. She hadn't seen a sign of Blake. The garage door was closed, so she couldn't tell if his car was in there or not. She stood by her car with the plans spread out on the bonnet, making a last-minute check. From there, she had a perfect vantage point to survey the work as a whole.

When she was through, she took up the plans and walked around to the pond at the back of the house. This part was all finished, but she wanted to double-check and make absolutely certain, since tomorrow was the last day the workmen would be there.

She stood near the edge of the pond where the ground began to fall away gradually towards the water, intent on her work. The sun was even brighter now, and she began to feel too warm in her light jacket. She laid the plans down on a large flat rock at the edge of the pond and, as she slipped off her jacket, she heard a voice call her name.

Startled, she looked up. Blake was standing above her at the railing of the large veranda, leaning over, a can of beer in his hand. He smiled at her and raised the can.

'Would you like a beer?'

'No, thanks,' she said. She picked up the plans

and held her jacket in the crook of her arm. 'I'm not very fond of beer.' She laughed. 'Besides, I have to drive home.'

'A Coke, then?'

She thought a minute. It sounded tempting. She was hot and dusty and a little tired from all the walking. Besides, she probably should let Blake know that it would be all right to let the workmen go tomorrow.

'Sounds good,' she said.

As she climbed the outside staircase up to the veranda, he vanished inside the house, and when she got there, he came back with a glass, a bottle of Coke and a tin of peanuts. She could see now that he had changed out of his work clothes into a pair of khaki shorts and a loose cotton shirt, which was unbuttoned to reveal a lot of broad, tanned chest.

'Sit down,' he said, gesturing to a chair.

He poured her Coke into the glass and handed it to her, then settled back into his chair. 'How's it going?' he asked. 'Think I can let the men go tomorrow as planned?'

'Yes, it's all moving on schedule.' She reached for her set of plans and rolled them out on the table. 'I'll give you a run-down on what's going on.'

He moved his chair closer to hers and leaned over the table, listening intently as she pointed out one area after another, explaining as she went what had been done and what she planned to do in the months ahead. He asked questions as she went along, and she tried to make her replies as thorough and clear as possible.

Finally, when he seemed satisfied, she glanced up and was startled to see that the sun was dipping quite low behind the tall evergreens at the western edge of the property. She glanced at her watch. It was almost seven o'clock. They'd been so absorbed in their discussion that two hours had flown by.

'I'd better be going,' she said, and started to get up. 'I had no idea it was so late.'

'It's Friday,' he said. 'You don't have to work tomorrow. What's the hurry?'

She was standing now and looked down at him in some confusion. 'I don't know.' She smiled. 'I guess I'm a little compulsive about time.'

'I know,' he said drily. 'Efficient, practical Jane.' He got up to stand beside her. 'Stay and have a little supper with me. There's some cold ham and potato salad in the fridge.'

She hesitated. Somehow the sight of those long straight legs, roughly covered with dark hair, and the bare, well-muscled chest, made her a little uneasy. She glanced up at him. He was smiling easily, the blue eyes thoughtful.

'All right,' she said. 'Just let me wash first.'

While Blake pottered in the kitchen getting out the food, dishes and silverware, Jane went along to the main bathroom off the hall. She knew from the tour of the house he had given her in May that he had his own private bath, and there wasn't a trace of him in this one, which was reserved for guests.

It was quite large, tiled in shades of dusty green and off-white, with a row of clean towels on the racks and a glass jar of coloured soap balls on the shelf by the sink. She set her bag down on the shelf and took off her blouse, then filled the basin with lukewarm water and gave her face and arms and upper body a good wash to clean off the dust and grime of the day.

When she had dried off, she gave her hair a good brushing and applied her usual trace of lipstick. As she gazed at her reflection, she suddenly became aware that she had worn only the sheer flesh-coloured teddy that morning under her clothes. It had been so foggy that she'd expected it to be cooler than it turned out to be, and she'd assumed she'd keep her jacket on all day.

That jacket was now hanging out on Blake's veranda where she'd left it. She hurriedly slipped on her blouse and buttoned it and looked again in the mirror. Her worst fears were confirmed when she saw that it appeared as though she wore absolutely nothing under the thin white blouse. She'd have to get back out to the veranda and get that jacket on, she thought. It would never do for Blake to see her like this. He'd think she was being deliberately provocative.

But when she went down the hall and back out on the veranda, her jacket was nowhere in sight. He must have hung it up while she was in the bathroom. Would it be too obvious if she asked him for it? She could tell him she was cold. It was still quite warm out, though, and if she made such a patently untrue statement, it would only draw attention to what she wanted to conceal.

Then she realised that the sun had gone down quite far beneath the trees, casting the house in shadows. Soon it would be dark. There was nothing to worry about. Besides, it suddenly occurred to her, she'd been sitting out there right next to him for two hours with her jacket off. Whatever there was to see, he'd already seen, and, she added wryly, it certainly hadn't sent him into transports of lust.

In a minute he came outside with a loaded tray.

She noticed that he'd buttoned his shirt, but he still looked half-naked with the bare tanned arms and rough legs still visible.

'Are you hungry?' he asked as he set the food out on the table.

'Yes, a little. This looks good.'

He had brought out a bottle of chilled white Bordeaux, and when he had filled their glasses, he lifted his in a toast.

'To the garden,' he said.

'The garden,' she repeated with a smile.

As they touched glasses lightly, their eyes met for a moment. Before he looked away, she saw his gaze flicker lower, but so briefly that she didn't have time to wonder if he'd noticed what the thin blouse so clearly revealed.

'Tell me,' he said, helping himself to the potato salad, 'how is the painting coming?'

'Quite well,' she said, glad of a safe neutral subject. 'I'm thinking about taking your advice and looking for a possible publisher when I get a collection together that satisfies me.'

'That's good,' he said. 'You have a real talent and should develop it.' He ate in silence for a few minutes, then said, 'How's Robert?'

'He's fine. Just back from depositions in Tucson.'

'So are you getting married after all?'

She sat stock still with her fork poised in mid-air and stared blankly at him. 'Married?'

He nodded. 'Wasn't that the plan?'

She set her fork down carefully and reached for her wine. 'No,' she said, taking a swallow. 'That's all off. Like I told you,' she amended, 'it was never really on. It wasn't in the cards.'

'I see,' he said slowly. 'As you know, I came to

pretty much the same conclusion about Monica.
We still see each other, but only as old friends.'

Then they weren't still engaged, she thought.
Her spirits soared.

'How is the Houston project going?' she asked.

'Quite well.' He pushed his plate away and lit a
cigarette. 'I have to go down there in a few weeks
to get the plans finalised. Then we should start
construction by October.'

'Does that mean you'll be moving down there?'
she asked, alarmed. Would he leave his house now
that the garden was so far along?

'For the winter, anyway, and possibly on into
the spring. It depends on the weather down there
and, of course, the labour situation. I don't intend
to move there permanently, if that's what you
mean, but I'll be spending most of my time in
Houston, probably for several months, possibly as
long as a year.'

Her heart sank as she realised how much she
would miss him. We're only friends, she reminded
herself. There's no commitment, not even a real
attachment. He'll get on with his life, and I'll get
on with mine, and that will be that.

She slowly rose to her feet. 'I guess I'd better be
going.'

'Wouldn't you like some coffee?' he asked. 'A
drink?'

'No, thanks.' She picked up her bag. 'The
dinner was lovely. Thank you very much.'

He had risen to stand beside her now. Dusk had
fallen, and high in the distant trees an owl hooted. It
was so still that she could hear the running water of
the creek and the crickets starting up their evening
chorus. A wave of such poignant sadness and
loneliness passed over her, that she felt close to tears.

She turned to him and forced out a bright smile.
He was gazing at her intently, a thoughtful look on
his face, the blue eyes unfathomable in the
shadows.

'I'll get your jacket, then,' he said quietly.

While she waited for him, she walked to the
edge of the veranda and stood gazing out at the
peaceful scene below. All the scars of the recent
excavations were shrouded in the gathering
darkness, now, and in her mind's eye she could
envisage the garden as it would look in the spring,
a spring without Blake. She shivered a little, and
didn't hear him come back until he spoke in a low
voice from behind her.

'Are you cold?' he asked.

Suddenly she couldn't speak. She could feel the
warmth of his body on her back, sense the hard-
muscled strength of him, and a surge of such
helpless longing at the thought of losing even the
little bit she had of him simply shook her to the very
depths. Before she could stop herself, her shoulders
began to shake and hot tears burned her eyes.

Then his hands were gripping her upper arms.
'Jane,' he said, bending over her. 'Jane, what is it?'

She wiped her eyes with the back of her hand
and shook her head helplessly. She didn't dare
speak for fear she'd break down completely. She
felt him hesitate for a moment, then he tightened
his hold on her and pulled her slowly back until
she rested against his hard body.

His arms came around to cross in front of her,
holding her, and he bent his head so that his
cheek was pressed up against hers. Jane sucked
in a deep breath of air and held it, hardly daring
to move, so filled with pleasurable sensations at
his touch, his voice, that she felt she could die

happy right on the spot.

He gently turned her round then. With one hand he cupped her chin, tilting her head up so that she gazed directly into his eyes, and with the other he smoothed back the hair from her forehead.

'I still want you, Jane,' he murmured. 'I've never stopped wanting you.'

With her head whirling and her pulses pounding, Jane stared at him through the mist of her tears. The blue gaze held her a willing prisoner as she tried to plumb their azure depths. His words had stunned her beyond belief. He still wants me, the voice in her head was singing, and a great warmth began to steal through her.

She sank pliantly against him and reached up to touch the fine mouth, tracing its outline with her fingertips as though to memorise it. Then his arms came around her and he kissed her with such force that the breath was almost knocked out of her. Gasping, she felt his mouth engulfing hers, his tongue pushing past her parted lips.

She was sinking, sinking slowly, down into a place of such bliss that she never wanted it to end. His hands were moving feverishly up and down her back now, sliding over the thin silk of her blouse, pulling it out of the waistband of her skirt, until she felt his palms on the silk at her waist.

He pulled his head back and stared down at her. 'I've waited so long for this,' he rasped. Then he smiled crookedly. 'You told me to be patient, and I've tried, but I can't wait for you any longer.' He put his hands on her hips and pulled her tightly to him. 'You see how I want you,' he whispered. 'Say you want me, too.'

She tried to think, to summon up her common sense, all the reasons she had decided were against exactly what was happening, but the only thought that came to her was that no force on earth could persuade her what she felt for this man could possibly be wrong.

She laid a hand on his cheek. 'Yes, Blake. Of course I want you.'

He drew slightly back from her and stood quite motionless for a while, just staring at her. It was almost dark now, but a light burning inside the house fell across his face so that it was just visible. She could scarcely take in the sheer beauty of the fine straight nose, the flat hollows of his lean cheeks, the wide bony jaw.

Then he reached out a hand and placed it at the side of her neck. Very slowly, he let it glide down until it rested on one breast, then just as slowly moved across to the other, leaving a trail of fire behind it. He raised his other hand and unfastened the row of buttons down the front of her blouse, separating it when he was through to reveal the wicked teddy underneath.

Slipping the blouse off her shoulders, he lowered his mouth to the deep shadow between her breasts. She threw her head back and felt his fingers lightly playing over her nipples and the soft flesh revealed by the plunging neckline of the scanty undergarment.

'You're so beautiful,' he murmured as he slipped one thin strap off her shoulder, then the other.

And at that moment she knew she *was* beautiful. She opened her eyes and watched the large brown hands move over her bare upper body, and she thought she'd never seen anything so breathtaking. When he bent down again to kiss first one firm breast, then trail his lips across to take the peak of the other into his hot moist mouth, she put her hands on his dark head and pulled him closer to her with a low moan of desire.

At the sound, he straightened up and unbuttoned his own shirt. She could hear his rasping breath, see the powerful shoulder muscles flex when he twisted sideways to drop the shirt on to a chair, then she let her eyes drop to his broad bare chest, his flat stomach, and the low-slung shorts, where a light sprinkling of dark hair appeared.

'Touch me,' he murmured.

She put both hands flat on his chest and ran them up over his shoulders, down his arms and back up again. As she trailed her fingers lower, she could feel the taut muscled flesh of his stomach quiver under her touch. With a groan deep in his throat, he pulled her roughly to him so that her breasts flattened against his chest, and she threw her arms around his neck.

He picked her up and started walking into the house with her. Her arms were still around his neck, her fingers twining through the thick hair at the back of it, her face pressed into the hollow of his throat. The smell and taste of his warm skin intoxicated her, and her mind was filled with only one thought: Blake *wants* me! Blake wants *me*!

He carried her into his darkened bedroom and set her down near the bed, then moved away from her to switch on a dim lamp beside it. The moment he left her, she felt suddenly chilled, lonely, and a little frightened. She watched the tall lithe body, loving it, wanting it still, but when he straightened up and started walking towards her again and she saw the burning, hungry look in his eyes, his hands at the waistband of his shorts, she realised that in a moment he would be standing naked before her, and she felt suddenly shy.

She crossed her arms in front of her. 'Blake,' she said in a faltering tone, and backed away a step from him.

Then he reached out and his arms came around her. 'What is it, Jane?'

She looked up into his eyes, trying to fathom what was going on behind them. 'Why, Blake?' she whispered. 'Why me? You can have your pick of women. Why do you need another conquest?'

He gave her a puzzled look. 'Conquest? Is that what you think?'

'Why, then?' she repeated. She had to know.

'Because you're you,' he said gravely. 'Because I care about you. I'm a man, you're a woman. Did you think we were just going to be pals, buddies, forever? Is that what you wanted?'

She knew it was no time to hedge or hide behind outraged virtue. Only complete honesty would do. She shook her head. 'No,' she said. 'You know it's not what I wanted. But I'm not sure I'm ready for this.'

His hands were kneading her shoulders gently, and he was gazing past her into the dark corners of the room, a thoughtful look on his face.

'I don't mean to rush you,' he said at last, looking down at her again. 'I think I've been very patient. I'm not just after a conquest. I don't operate that way. I care about *you*, as a person. Your talent, your intelligence, your good sense. I *like* you, Jane, very much.'

She was warming again under his touch, reassured by his nearness, and she believed him. What bothered her was the future. Where would it lead? What could she count on from him. Could she sleep with him without any kind of commitment?

His hands were travelling on her body now, moving slowly and lightly from her shoulders down over her breasts, her waist, and slipping below the waistband of her skirt to press against her flat stomach. He put his mouth at her ear.

'Is it wrong,' he murmured, 'to care about your beautiful body, too?' He raised his head and gazed down into her eyes. 'We've got a good thing going for us, Jane. I don't know where it will lead, but it won't lead anywhere if you're afraid of your feelings for me or don't trust me.'

Her feelings for him were absolutely clear in her mind. She loved him, probably always had since the moment they met, with every fibre of her being, and yes, she was afraid of the consuming power of those feelings. But she knew now that, coming this far, she couldn't back out.

She smiled at him. 'No,' she said, 'it's not wrong.'

She put her arms around him and raised her head for his kiss. As his mouth covered hers, warm and seeking, he undid her skirt and pushed it down over her hips until it lay on the floor at her feet. His hands came back up over her legs, reaching under the brief bikini underpants to pull them off, too.

This time, when he undid his shorts and stepped out of them, she didn't back down, but only gazed with adoration at the long, powerfully male body that was revealed to her. When they came together again, bare flesh on bare flesh, all thought ceased, and the most overpowering sensations she'd ever known consumed her mind, her body, her very being.

He eased her down on top of the bed and hovered over her, his elbows supporting him, as he made slow deliberate love to her. His hands and mouth were everywhere, awakening responses in her that left her gasping and helpless. She clutched frantically at him, his head, his shoulders, his narrow hips, wanting him closer, longing to have him inside her now to ease the fiery ache that was driving her wild.

Finally, he raised his head and gazed deeply into her eyes. He kissed her eyelids, her cheeks, her chin, then took her mouth in a passionate demanding kiss and lowered himself on to her so that they were joined together at last. As he moved within her, she felt one sharp jab of pain, then an intensity of pleasure that built and built in a rising crescendo until she cried out, digging her fingers into his broad back as wave after wave of glorious release flooded through her.

Just as she began to come slowly down to earth again, she felt him shake with a mighty spasm, then, groaning, he pressed his head into her shoulder and his mouth opened on her throat. They clung together for a long time until finally their breathing returned to normal. He slid off her, his head still buried in her neck, and sighed deeply.

In a moment or two his breathing became deep and regular, and she realised that he must be asleep. She sank back into the pillow and closed her eyes, simply allowing herself to enjoy the sheer pleasure of the feel of his body lying next to her. It was indescribable, she thought, and wondered how she could have gone for so long without experiencing this, the greatest joy in life.

The answer was clear. She hadn't met Blake Bannister before. No matter what happened, she vowed silently, she'd always be grateful to him for the precious gift he had given her. She felt him shift slightly at her side then, and glanced over at him.

He was on his back now, one arm flung over his head, the other still around her neck. She wanted to memorise every inch of him. He seemed so vulnerable to her in sleep, and this gave her an odd sense of possession, as though he really belonged to her. And he does, she thought fiercely, if only for a short time.

She longed to touch him, but didn't want to wake him. She inched her hand slowly towards the bedside lamp to switch it off, and as she did, the arm around her neck tightened, and she felt him roll over to curl against her.

'Stay the night,' he murmured sleepily against the back of her neck.

Both arms came around her then, and when she turned off the light, she felt his hands cover her breasts, then slide lower over her ribcage, her stomach, her thighs, then back up again where his fingers began to play lightly, lazily with her taut nipples.

They made slow love again in the darkness, then, satisfied at last, they got under the covers and slept in each other's arms.

The next morning they showered together, then had breakfast out on the veranda. Jane had wanted to leave before the workmen came, but Blake protested so vehemently that she finally decided that at this point it really didn't matter who saw them together.

Besides, she wanted to stay. Just watching him across the table at breakfast in the early morning light thrilled her to the core after what had passed between them last night. She could never get enough of just looking at him. Watching the large brown hands that held the cup as he drank his coffee and remembering how those same hands had held her last night so intimately, brought a flush to her cheeks, and she dropped her eyes away.

'Any regrets, Jane?' he asked softly. He reached out and covered her hand lying on the table with his.

He'd noticed her embarrassment, she thought, and forced herself to meet his gaze. Once again, she was dazzled by the deep blue of his eyes, but his expression was thoughtful and genuinely concerned.

'No, of course not.'

'Good,' he said. 'It was the first time for you, wasn't it?'

She lifted her chin. 'Yes. Does that bother you?'

He chuckled. 'Not in the slightest. I'm honoured. Most men will claim it doesn't matter these days, but, believe me, it does.'

He drained his coffee in one long swallow, then got up and came to stand behind her chair. He bent over and crossed his arms in front of her, brushing against her breasts, then cupping them, weighing them in his hands.

The intimate gesture out there on the veranda in broad daulight with the workmen due any minute brought the fire to her cheeks again. She twisted her head around to remonstrate with him, but before she could speak, he had covered her mouth softly with his own. With his tongue gliding tantalisingly over her lips and one hand now slipping inside her blouse, she couldn't speak. She was lost, and she knew it.

'Let's go to bed,' he murmured against her

mouth, and when he stood back and held out a hand to her, the blue eyes alight with naked desire, she took it helplessly, rose from her seat and allowed him to lead her inside the house.

CHAPTER NINE

THE next two weeks were the happiest of Jane's life. She was simply, deliriously and totally in love. In her rare moments of calm sanity, away from him, she would try to summon up all her old practical common sense, telling herself sternly, as she weeded her garden or sat at her desk in the office, that it was not going to last, that she must prepare herself for the day when he would be gone out of her life.

It was no use. She'd find herself sitting on the grass, trowel in hand, the garden forgotten, her mind filled with the memory of how his mouth felt on hers, his body pressed against her, his hands moving hotly over her, and she'd be lost. Finally, she just gave up. When the blow came she'd just have to deal with it the best she could.

He never spoke a word of love. In the small hours of the night he would whisper to her that her body set him on fire or that he was crazy about her, or other small endearments. She never doubted again that he found her intensely desirable, even though she still couldn't understand why. He was a very affectionate person, and when they were out together, he touched her constantly, holding her hand as they walked down a street, putting his arm around her in a darkened theatre.

He was a bold, daring lover, and although in the beginning it made her a little nervous, she soon came to enjoy his demonstrations of affection in the most unlikely places. They were further proof

of his genuine attraction to her. In fact, he made
her feel so desirable and cherished that she literally
glowed. Randi had been giving her strangely
assessing looks lately, and she knew it was only a
matter of time before she was confronted with the
demand for an explanation as to why she was
smiling all the time these days.

Although they never talked about it, she knew
he would be leaving for Houston soon. Two
weeks, he'd said that first night at his house. She
tried not to think about it, but finally the time
came when she had to face it.

They'd gone to a movie downtown, then
driven out to Alki Point in West Seattle to a
small cocktail lounge for a drink afterwards. It
was built on the very edge of a high bluff
overlooking the Sound, and they had been seated
side by side facing a window. Down below, the
light from an incoming ferry glowed against the
black water.

They had sat in silence for some time, sipping
their drinks, so close together that Jane could feel
the hard length of his thigh pressed against hers,
warming her. She was filled with contentment just
to be with him. Then she felt his hand on her
bare knee, squeezing it gently.

'I'm leaving for Houston the day after tomorrow,' he said quietly.

For a moment her heart simply stopped beating.
She put her hand over his and turned to him.

'So soon?' She sighed. 'I was hoping . . .'

He nodded and took a sip of his drink. 'I know.'
Then he turned to her. 'Come with me, Jane.'

Her mouth fell open. 'Come with you?' she said
blankly. The hand on her knee began sliding up
and down the inside of her thigh, and she was

having trouble thinking straight. 'How can I do that?'

'Just come,' he said. 'We can find an apartment, you can do your painting.'

'You mean, get married?'

The minute the words were out of her mouth she regretted them. The hand stilled on her leg, then withdrew. He lit a cigarette and leaned a little away from her, frowning straight ahead at the smoke.

'You already know how I feel about that,' he said finally. He looked at her. 'I care about you, I really do. But to me, marriage is for ever, and a permanent commitment just isn't in the cards for me. Not now, not the way I live.'

She smiled brightly and put a hand on his arm. 'I know,' she said. 'You just took me so by surprise that I didn't know what to think, what you were talking about.' She laughed and squeezed his arm. 'That wasn't a proposal, only a request for information. I'm no more ready to settle down than you are.'

It was a barefaced lie, but she had no choice. He looked a little surprised for a moment, but then he relaxed visibly, stubbed out his cigarette and smiled.

'Well, that's all right, then. Will you come?'

'I don't see how I can, Blake. I've got my job and the house to take care of.'

'Will you think about it, at least?' He put his hand on her cheek. 'I don't want to lose you, honey,' he said softly.

She almost gave in right then and there and said she'd go with him under any conditions. Almost. But her good sense warned her to wait before making a definite decision. There was plenty of time.

'Yes, of course,' she said. 'I'll think about it.'

They didn't speak again of his request, although Jane had thought of nothing else since he'd mentioned it. She was absolutely torn in two. The thought of leaving her job, her home, her friends, her pleasant sensible safe life, was simply inconceivable to her. Yet to give up this chance of being with the man she loved seemed even worse.

The next night, their last together, she decided that, if he pressed the issue, she would agree. The very thought of his leaving was so painful to her that she thought she would have agreed to anything, and for once in her life kicked over the traces to do something totally out of character, just so she wouldn't lose him.

They were lying side by side in Blake's big bed. The curtains were drawn, and a full moon lit up the room with a pale, silvery glow. They had just made love, and Jane was on her back, her eyes closed, utterly spent and basking in the afterglow of passion.

She felt Blake shift his position so that he was on his side facing her. His hand settled on her stomach, and he buried his face in her shoulder with his mouth at her neck. She listened for a while to the quiet breathing that told her he was asleep, then opened her eyes to gaze down at him.

He was even more beautiful in sleep, she thought. Cautiously, so as not to waken him, she raised a hand and placed it on the dark head, smoothing the tousled hair back from his forehead. She looked down at the long length of him. The strong body gleamed palely in the moonlight, and she wanted to memorise everything about him, his clean distinctive scent, the feel of

the thick crisp hair under her fingers, the taste of
his mouth and skin.

As though sensing her concentration, he stirred
slightly in his sleep, murmuring against her neck.
The hand on her stomach moved up to settle on
her breast, his grip tightening possessively, then
relaxing to lie there, strong and brown, against her
pale skin.

Ask me again to go with you, Blake, she said to
herself, and I'll do it. Even as she thought it,
though, she knew he wouldn't. To go even that
far, considering his rejection of any kind of
commitment, was a major concession to his need
of her, and he wouldn't press it.

Besides, she thought a little ruefully, I'm the one
who's taught him to be patient, and I'll just have
to make the decision on my own.

She drove him to the airport early the next
morning. They misjudged the timing and almost
missed the plane. They only had time for a
hurried, last-minute kiss before he had to run
down the ramp where they were just closing the
gate.

'I'll call you tonight,' he said as he moved away
from her, and then he was gone.

I didn't really even say goodbye to him, she
thought sadly as she drove home on the near-
empty Sunday morning streets. In the car that
morning, he'd said he'd be able to come to Seattle
at least twice a month to check on the downtown
construction. That wasn't so bad.

Her house seemed cold and barren without him.
In the past two weeks he'd spent as much time at
her place as she had at his. She set down her bag
and wandered through the rooms, searching for

some trace of him. He'd left a shirt in her bedroom. She picked it up, buried her face in it, and had a good, half-hour cry. When it was over, she washed her face, put on her oldest clothes and went out to attack her neglected garden.

When he called that night, she felt like sobbing with relief the minute she heard his voice. Instead, she calmed herself and spoke as cheerfully and composedly as she could.

'Blake, I'm so glad you arrived safely. Where are you?'

'In a hotel in the middle of Houston at the moment,' he said. 'I'll rent a car tomorrow and look for something a little more permanent.'

'You sound tired.'

'I'm wiped out. I got here around noon and have been in meetings ever since. I'm about ready to shower and sack out.'

'Sounds like a good idea.'

'Jane,' he said, lowering his voice, 'I miss you already.'

'Oh, Blake, I miss you, too.'

'I'm lying on top of the bed,' he went on dreamily, 'and when I close my eyes I can almost imagine you're here beside me.'

Her heart turned over, and a familiar warmth began to radiate through her. 'Don't, Blake,' she murmured.

'Do you know what I'm thinking about now?'

'No.'

'Do you remember our last night, when you woke me up . . .'

'*I* woke *you* up?'

'Well, whatever. Anyway, it was right after the episode in the shower. Or was it before?'

'Blake!' she cried, her cheeks burning. 'Not on the telephone!'

He laughed. 'All right, my sensible little Jane. I'll let you go before I really embarrass you. I may not be able to call you for a while, but I'll let you know as soon as I can how it's coming.' He paused. 'I hope you'll consider coming down here. Just for a visit,' he added hastily. 'I'm not going to push you.'

After they hung up, Jane sat with her hand on the telephone, as though somehow that brought him nearer. God, how she missed him! He'd only been gone a day. What would it be like after a week? Two weeks? Maybe a month.

Should she go down there, just for a visit? Everything in her wanted to, but somehow the idea of actually getting on a plane, going to Houston, staying with him, bothered her. It was one thing to carry on a secret romance right here in Seattle, where she had her own home, but quite another to flaunt their affair publicly.

For some reason, she thought for the first time of what her father would say. They'd always been close, and she knew he was proud of her sensible, no-nonsense approach to life. A typical engineer, it was his way, too. What would he say if he knew she was thinking about traipsing off to a strange city to live openly with a man who had no intention of offering her marriage? She couldn't do it, she decided, and that was that.

She missed Blake far more than she had even dreamed she would. In just two short weeks he had taken over her life, her mind, her emotions, to the point where without him she felt like half a person.

She tried to keep busy. The day after he left, she made herself go through the stack of watercolours and ink drawings she'd done in the past, and she finally gathered a respectable collection together, one that she wouldn't be ashamed to present to a prospective publisher.

The following morning before work, she wrapped the collection securely and then, in her lunch hour, she dropped them off at a local publishing house she had decided might be interested in printing them. On her way back to the office, she gazed up at the building next door, still under construction. Blake's building. The sign was still there out in front, *Bannister Construction Company*. But Blake wasn't there. It was almost finished now, at least the shell, and the show out of the twentieth floor window was over.

Randi was alone in the long room when Jane got back. The models would be out of town for the next week on an assignment for another magazine, and it was very quiet. Jane missed their chatter more than she would have thought possible. She even missed the pounding and sawing next door.

'Well?' Randi said, looking up at her from her desk as Jane passed by. 'How's it going?' She leaned back in her chair and eyed Jane narrowly. 'Is something wrong?'

Jane smiled. 'No, nothing's wrong. Why do you ask?'

Randi shrugged. 'Oh, I don't know. It's just that in the past couple of weeks you seemed to be so happy. You were blossoming into a real beauty, as a matter of fact. I've never seen you look so alive and happy.' She smiled wryly. 'There's only one thing I know of that can do that to a woman, and that's a man.'

Jane reddened and turned to walk over to her desk. She was tempted to confide in her friend, just to get some help in sorting out her own confused emotional state, but the habit of reserve was so strong in her that she couldn't bring herself to discuss this, the most overwhelming experience of her life. She stood at her desk and fiddled nervously with the papers lying on top of it.

Randi had got up and followed her. She stood in front of Jane's desk now, facing her, her hands on her hips, her head cocked to one side in a long, appraising glance.

'I knew it couldn't be Robert,' she went on, 'not after all these years.' She shrugged. 'So I figured it must be the gorgeous hunk next door, your new "employer", Blake Bannister.' She shook her head admiringly. 'I've got to hand it to you, kiddo, you walked off with a real prize.'

Jane didn't know what to say. What could she say? She couldn't deny Randi's conclusions about her relationship with Blake, but she still felt she couldn't discuss it with anyone. All her life she'd made her own decisions, reasoned out her problems, then acted on them. The habit was too strong to break lightly.

When she didn't speak, Randi made an offhand gesture in the air with one perfectly manicured hand. 'Guess it's none of my business,' she said. 'But in the last few days that nice glow of yours has disappeared, and I just thought . . .' Her voice trailed off and she started to turn away.

'Randi,' Jane called to her. 'Randi, I don't know what to do. I feel as though I'm being torn apart.' Randi turned and gave her an enquiring gaze. 'You're right about Blake,' Jane went on, lowering her eyes, 'I'm in love with him.'

'That's great!' Randi said. 'And I take it the feeling is mutual.' She sighed deeply. 'Lucky you.' Then she frowned. 'Or are you? What's the problem?'

'He'll be in Houston for several months on a new job, and he wants me to go with him,' Jane blurted out.

'Well?' Randi said. 'When are you leaving?'

'Randi, I can't. I just can't go.'

'Why on earth not?' Randi looked so surprised that Jane had to search her mind carefully before she answered.

'Well, I just can't. I have my job, my house. I can't just pick up and follow him half-way across the country.'

Randi placed the palms of her hands flat on the desk, leaned over and stared straight into Jane's eyes.

'If you don't,' she said in a firm tone, 'you're crazy. I'd walk barefoot to Houston for a chance at a man like Blake Bannister.'

'I can't risk it,' Jane said weakly. 'He doesn't want any commitments.'

'So?' Randi raised her eyebrows.

'So, a relationship without commitment frightens me.'

Randi thought this over for a minute. 'OK,' she said at last. 'Knowing you, I can understand that. You're probably right. But just remember one thing. If you go, you do risk getting your heart broken. There are no guarantees he'll wake up some morning and decide he can't live without you. But on the other hand, if you don't go, you'll surely lose him. A man like that isn't going to hang around unattached for ever. Take your choice.'

'Some choice,' Jane grumbled.

'That's life, kiddo,' Randi said with a laugh. 'Think it over anyway,' she added in a kinder tone.

'That's all I've been doing.' Then she smiled. 'But thanks, Randi. It helps to talk it out with someone.'

'Any time, kiddo,' Randi went back to her own desk. 'Any time.'

For the next week, Jane thought about nothing else. She went through her daily chores like an automaton, but he was constantly on her mind. As the days passed and he didn't call, she found herself leaning more and more towards taking the risk, giving up the nice safe life, just to be with him.

She began to worry that he'd changed his mind, and even half-convinced herself that it had all been a dream. When she thought about him, his good looks, his self-assurance, his intensely masculine appeal, all their moments together, she found it harder and harder to believe that he really wanted her.

On Friday, the publishing company where she'd left her paintings called her at work, full of enthusiasm for the collection and anxious to discuss terms with her. She made an appointment to go in on Monday to talk it over. When she'd hung up, Jane just sat at her desk for a long time mulling over this latest development. She was thrilled, of course, that an objective critic had seen value in her work, but much more than that, she saw it as a sign.

If I can start selling my paintings, she thought, it won't be so hard to give up my job. And, she went on, if I can give up my job, there's no practical reason why I shouldn't go to Houston to be with Blake.

Still, he didn't call, and by Sunday night, she was almost frantic. She didn't feel yet that she'd come to a definite decision. She couldn't do that until she heard his voice again, knew he still wanted her. Maybe he'd never call. Maybe it was already too late.

She'd sat by the phone all evening, waiting for it to ring, until finally, disgusted with herself, she decided to go out into the garden and get an early start on her autumn pruning. She worked listlessly for half an hour, and then she heard the telephone ring.

By the time she'd run into the house to answer it, she was out of breath. It had rung five times, and she was terrified he'd hang up before she got there. She snatched up the receiver.

'Hello,' she said breathlessly.

'Hi,' he said, 'it's me.'

'Blake,' she said simply, and sank with relief into the chair by the telephone stand. It was so wonderful just to hear his voice again, exactly as she remembered it, deep and warm and inviting.

'Sorry I haven't called sooner,' he went on, 'but I've been virtually living out on the site, and this is the first breather I've had.'

'How does it look?' She'd got her breath back by now and was able to make her voice steady, in spite of her weak knees and thudding heart.

'Great,' he replied. 'It's all going like clockwork so far.' He paused, then lowered his voice intimately. 'God, I've missed you, honey.'

A great lump formed in Jane's throat at the words. 'I've missed you, too,' she said shakily.

'Have you come to a decision yet?' he asked. He

laughed briefly. 'I'm trying to be patient, but I want you here with me. Badly.'

For one moment, she hesitated. Her heart beat faster, her mind raced, and she had a strong sensation of dizziness, as though she were about to plunge off a high cliff into a cold sea. Then, suddenly, she was filled with certainty.

'Yes, Blake,' she said calmly. 'I've made up my mind. I want to come. I want to be with you.'

She heard him expel a deep breath. 'You won't be sorry, darling. I promise you, you won't be sorry. When can you get here?'

'I think it would be best for me to come for a visit first,' she said. 'I have to decide what to do about the house, and I can't just leave the magazine in the lurch. I have to wait until they find a replacement for me.'

He sighed. 'All right,' he agreed. 'You're still my practical Jane, and I guess I'm stuck with you the way you are. I'll settle for a visit this time, and we can look for an apartment together, but I'm going to insist on a permanent move very soon.'

Permanent? she thought after they'd hung up. How permanent? Not very, she was afraid. She wouldn't think about that. She'd made up her mind, committed herself, and she'd just do it.

Suddenly, there were so many things to be done that her head began to whirl. Her parents would have to know, for one thing, since she'd be leaving the house empty. Somehow that fact had escaped her attention while she was arriving at her decision. What would they say when she told them she was quitting her job, closing up the house and flying off to a strange city to be with a man they'd never even met?

Then she thought, I'm twenty-six years old.

What difference does it make what my parents think, for heaven's sake? I'm a mature, responsible adult. Besides, she added a little guiltily, maybe I won't tell them that part just yet.

She did, however, feel she should call them to let them know she would be gone the next weekend in case they tried to get her, but there was no hurry about that, either. She'd call them on Friday night, at the last minute. That was time enough.

The week passed in such a daze of hectic activity that Jane didn't have a moment to reconsider or regret her decision. Stan, her boss, was appalled when she told him she was quitting her job on the magazine, but was somewhat mollified when she assured him she would stay until he found a replacement for her. He even ended up by congratulating her when she told him about the proposed book, and agreed with her that she should spend more time on her own work.

By Friday night, she was all packed and ready to leave first thing in the morning. All that remained for her to do was to call her parents in Florida to tell them she'd be out of town for a few days. Perhaps she could even prepare them for the fact that she planned to go to Houston to stay later on. Certainly she'd have to discuss with them what they wanted her to do about the house.

It had been on her mind all day. Now that the rush of the week was over, and she really was all set to go, she knew she'd have to face this last unpleasant task. She'd already committed herself. Blake would be at the airport in Houston to meet her early the next afternoon. She'd burned her bridges at the magazine. Now all that remained was to tell her parents.

She put it off all evening, delaying the moment of actually going to the telephone and placing the call with a dozen little unnecessary tasks. Finally, she sat down on the chair beside the telephone stand and reached for the receiver, when it suddenly rang.

It was Robert. 'I haven't talked to you for some time,' he said. 'Just thought I'd call to see how you were.'

Hearing his voice for the first time in weeks, she suddenly realised how much she'd missed her old friend and how glad she was to hear his familiar voice again.

'I thought you might like to drive over to the ocean with me on Sunday,' he went on. 'I've met a girl,' he hurried on before she could speak. 'I'd like to have you meet her.'

'Oh, Robert, I'm sorry, I can't! I'll be out of town. But tell me about her. Is it serious?'

'I'm not sure. I think it might be. I'd really like to have you meet her, kind of give her your seal of approval.' He laughed deprecatingly. 'We've been buddies for so long, you and I, that it wouldn't feel right making a serious move without consulting you. Maybe we can get together when you come back.'

'Yes, I'd like that.' She was deeply touched by his confidence in her, yet couldn't help feeling a sharp twinge of guilt at how much she'd hidden from him.

'Where are you going?' he asked. 'Any place exciting?'

'Houston,' she said shortly.

'Houston?' He sounded surprised. 'I didn't know you had friends in Houston. Or is it business?'

'Oh, Robert,' she said, annoyed, 'you don't have to know everything about me.'

There was a short, hurt silence. Then he said, 'Well, sure, Jane. You're right. I'm sorry.'

She was immediately contrite. 'I'm sorry, too, Robert, really I am. I shouldn't have snapped at you like that. I've been awfully busy lately, though, and had a lot on my mind.'

'Sure,' he said again, 'I understand.'

'I'll call you when I get back. I want to meet your friend.'

Now why, she asked herself when they'd hung up, did I do that? Robert hadn't been out of line. It was a perfectly natural question for one friend to ask another. What was the reason for her sudden burst of irritation?

She got up and walked slowly out into the garden. It had showered lightly that afternoon, but now, in the early evening, the sun had come out again, and the grass sparkled with raindrops. She paced up and down the paths, thinking about Robert, about what she hadn't told him, hadn't wanted to tell him, and about what she dreaded telling her parents.

After a good hour of this, she gradually had to face the fact that she was ashamed of what she was planning to do. It wasn't that she was afraid of what her parents would think. She knew them. Even if they were disappointed in her, they'd never say anything. It wasn't that Robert would condemn her, either. He'd told her about his own little fling in Los Angeles months ago, and wouldn't hold it against her that she was doing the same thing. Their friendship was an equal one, without any archaic double standard or undertone of masculine superiority.

She was simply ashamed. As she walked in the gathering dusk, she knew for a certainty that she wanted Blake Bannister more than she'd ever wanted anything in her life. The joy of his desiring her, caring for her, wanting her to be with him, was overwhelming to her. There was only one thing more important, she thought sadly, as she went back inside the house. Her own self-respect.

I'll never recover from this, she thought despairingly as she lifted the receiver of the telephone. She dialled slowly the number Blake had given her of his hotel.

CHAPTER TEN

HER announcement was met with a cold, stony silence. She waited for what seemed like an eternity, until finally she couldn't stand it another second.

'Blake? Are you there?'

'Yes,' he said stiffly, 'I'm still here. Do you mean you're not coming tomorrow for the weekend, or that you're not coming at all, ever?'

'Both, I guess.' He sounded so distant. But, then, what did she expect? She cleared her throat. 'I've decided I can't come to Houston to live with you, and so I think it's best not to come for a visit.'

'I see. And what brought about this decision?'

'Blake, please try to understand.' She was close to tears. 'I don't want to lose you, but I know I'd be miserable if I came down there as your—your . . .' She broke off, unable to think of a word that would describe her fears. 'And I'd end by making you miserable, too. I can't come down there and just move in with you.'

'Jane,' he said patiently, warming a little, 'it's done all the time nowadays. There's no stigma attached to it. No one will think a thing about it, or any the less of you.'

'I know that, and I've never condemned the women who choose that path.' She thought of Randi and Jennifer and Stephanie, all of whom had had live-in men friends since she'd known them. 'It's fine for them, it just wouldn't work for me.'

There was another long silence. 'What do you propose, then?' he asked at last.

'Well, you said you'd be coming home for occasional visits, and the job in Houston won't last for ever. Besides,' she said with a nervous laugh, 'I want to be here when they start planting your garden next month.'

'The hell with the garden,' he growled. 'I want you here with me now.'

She began to grow angry, then. She had expected him to be disappointed, as she was herself, but his tone of irate lover sounded almost childish, certainly high-handed and dictatorial.

'Well, I want to be with you, too,' she said, her voice rising. 'But not as your live-in pet.'

'Is that what you think it would be?' he said in an even, almost menacing tone.

'I don't know what it would be,' she replied curtly. 'I've never had any experience with this kind of arrangement, and I don't think I want to try it.'

'Then I guess there's nothing more to say, Jane. I think I knew all along you'd never actually go through with it. You're too sensible and practical to take a risk like that, aren't you?'

'Maybe so,' she said, hurt at his sarcastic tone. 'I just know I can't do it.'

'It's your decision, of course. There's no way I can force you against your will. I'm sorry, Jane. It could have been great for us.'

Her heart caught in her throat at his words. He made it sound so final. She was just about to ask him when he thought he'd be back for a visit, when he spoke again.

'I have to hang up now, Jane. There's someone at the door.'

They said their stiff goodbyes, then, and as she slowly hung up the receiver, she felt colder and lonelier than she ever had in her life. Before Blake, she'd been alone, but she'd come to terms with it, learned to live with it. Now, after his vibrant presence, his warmth, it was far worse, and she wasn't sure she had the strength to pick up the pieces again.

During the next two weeks, he was all she thought of. Randi's words of warning burned in her brain, haunting her every waking moment. 'A man like that isn't going to hang around unattached for ever.' She knew it was true, and a dozen times she'd been tempted to change her mind, to call him and ask him if he still wanted her.

She didn't hear from him at all, and after another long week of silence, she knew she wouldn't, that it was over. Her self-respect was cold comfort, she thought in the small hours of the morning when she couldn't sleep, compared to what she had lost. Now it was too late.

As the days passed, however, and she still had no word from him, she began to feel more angry than hurt. That helped a little towards easing the pain of loss in her heart. After all, she thought, she hadn't rejected him or ended their affair. He'd done that himself, just because he couldn't have his own way. Gradually, she came to be convinced that he'd never really cared for her or really wanted her in the first place. How could he, when at the first setback to *his* plans, *his* wishes, he simply vanished?

It was early October now, and time to start the planting on his property. The contract had been let in July, to a nursery in Woodinville Jane had done business with in the past, and several plants were due to be delivered on the third of the month, which fell on a Monday.

She had been in a state of constant internal warfare for days over whether she should go out to his place in Fall City to supervise the planting, as planned. She knew it would only open the old wound for her to see it again, but she'd taken on the responsibility, and she couldn't just leave the stock out there unplanted. Finally, by that Sunday night, she decided she'd just have to go through with it.

Early the next morning, she dressed in her shabbiest work clothes, stowed her garden tools in the car and started out on the familiar drive towards the mountains. It was a beautiful early autumn day, so crisp and clear that the new snow on the higher peaks gleamed like a field of diamonds in the distance. The leaves were turning now on the birch and alder and maple trees, and the winding road that led to Blake's house was lined with their flaming reds, oranges and yellows.

The nursery truck was already there when she pulled up in front of the house. She had arranged with the owner to send his teenage son out to help her do the planting. She couldn't do it all alone, even though this was only a partial shipment of the evergreens. The deciduous shrubs would have to wait until November when their leaves had completely dropped.

She greeted the boy, and they started immediately. He did all the heavy digging where she marked the spots, and by two o'clock they had placed all the plants in their permanent locations. She thanked him and, after he'd left, she wandered around surveying the day's work with a com-

bination of exhaustion and satisfaction. It was still
nowhere near completed, but the settled beds had
begun to take on the look of the garden she had
envisaged when she first started planning it, now
that the rhododendrons and azaleas were in.

The pond area looked especially nice, she
thought, as she inspected the work they'd done at
the back of the house. With the autumn rains, the
creek had risen, and the water was so clear she
could see the large smooth stones on the bottom.
As she walked, she found herself glancing up at
the overhanging veranda of the house from time to
time, and she recalled with a sudden great surge of
longing the meals she and Blake had shared out
there and that first night when he'd kissed her and
told her he wanted her.

No! she said to herself sternly, and began to
march purposefully towards the front of the house
where she'd parked her car. She was hot and tired
and filthy from her morning's labours. She was
also feeling very hungry.

'I made my choice,' she muttered grimly as she
trudged round the side of the house. And I'll stick
to it, she added silently.

Just as she came into view of the driveway, she
saw a taxi coming down the road towards the
house. She stood there, some hundred feet away,
rooted to the spot, her arms rigid at her sides, as
she watched a tall man dressed in a dark business
suit and carrying a suitcase step out. The cab
turned around then and drove away.

Blake! Jane couldn't move. Three weeks, she
thought, three long weeks without a word, and
now he picks the one day when I have to be here
to come home. And I still want him, she added
brokenly as he began to walk towards her in his

familiar confident, long stride.

She held up a hand in a reflex action, as though to stop him from coming nearer, and they both stood motionless, just staring, for a full minute. In that time, Jane found the strength to collect herself, and even though her heart was tripping all over itself in erratic beats, and her legs threatened to buckle under her, she made herself lift her chin, square her shoulders and move forward.

'Hello, Blake,' she said calmly as she approached him. 'As you can see, we went ahead with the planting on schedule.'

He continued to stare at her for some moments, then said, 'Yes, I see.'

She *wished* he wouldn't stare like that. She was suddenly acutely conscious of how she must look in her old jeans, crusted now with mud, and her sweaty shirt with the long tails hanging out. Her hair was mussed, she had no make-up on, and her hands were filthy.

Then she thought, what difference does it make? It's over. 'I wasn't sure whether you wanted me to go ahead with it or not,' she said aloud. 'But since the plans were all made with the nursery, I decided I should see it through.'

He still didn't say anything. Perhaps he's decided to give me the silent treatment, she thought. Very well, she decided, I've already lost him, so I have nothing to gain by standing here like an idiot waiting for him to say something. She walked over to her car and put her hand on the latch of the door.

'I'll be on my way,' she said. 'If you have any further orders, you can call me,' and she opened the car door.

'Jane,' he said. He set his suitcase down and

took the few steps that separated them until he was standing before her. 'Jane,' he repeated, staring down at her.

She couldn't look at him. Her one thought was to get away before she made a fool of herself. His nearness was making her head swim, and she knew that one glance into those dazzling blue eyes and she'd be lost, would agree to anything, and then have to go through the whole painful process again.

'I have to go now,' she said gruffly, and pulled the car door open wider.

Then she felt his hand on her shoulder. She shivered under his touch and bowed her head as she felt the tears sting her eyes. She *would* not let him see her cry. She tried to pull away from him, but he held her firmly.

Then he put his other hand on her shoulder and forced her gently around to face him. Summoning up all her strength, she gazed up at him. There was a look in his eyes, a softness around his mouth, that she'd never seen before. He shook his head slowly from side to side and smiled crookedly.

'I don't know whatever made me think I could live without you,' he said in a low husky voice.

'Oh, Blake, don't,' she pleaded. 'Please don't.'

The tears spilled over, then, and he gathered her into his arms, holding her close, smoothing back her hair as she sobbed into his chest, and making soothing noises as he stroked her. When she had quietened down, she looked up at him.

'I've ruined your shirt,' she sniffed. She ran a hand over her hair. 'I'm such a mess.'

'You're beautiful,' he said, with feeling. He held her away from him and glanced up and down her body. 'You know what I see whenever I look at you or think about you?'

'What?' she whispered. She felt as though she was choking.

'I see you in that fetching little wisp of skin-coloured lace and silk. You know the one?'

'Blake,' she said, staring at him helplessly.

'But it's more than that,' he went on. 'It's you, who you are, your strength, your intelligence, your character, that are even more important than how you look, and I finally see that. In a word, I love you no matter what.'

Her eyes widened. 'What did you say?'

'I love you,' he said gravely. 'I love you, Jane. I thought I could get along without you, but I can't. It's as simple as that.'

'But,' she protested, 'you haven't called, haven't written. I thought . . .'

He kissed her lightly on the mouth. 'I know what you thought. I thought the same thing. It was over. Then, as I missed you more each day, I began to see that it was only over because I didn't get *my* way, because you wouldn't fall in with *my* plans.' He shrugged helplessly. 'When you refused to come to Houston, I guess I figured you didn't care for me as I cared for you.'

'Oh, no,' she cried. 'It was never that.' She put a hand on his cheek. 'I've loved you from the day we met, when I fell into your arms down in Pioneer Square on Fat Tuesday. I'm just such a coward, I was afraid to go to you in Houston.

'No, darling. I was the coward, not you. I was asking you to take all the chances, and I wasn't willing to risk a thing.' A broad smile lit up his face then, and the blue eyes blazed down at her. 'But now it's all right. We'll get married and *then* you'll come to Houston with me.' His eyes clouded. 'Won't you?'

She simply couldn't speak. Married? To Blake? To spend the rest of her life with him, to have his children. It was more than she could comprehend.

'Jane,' he said sternly, giving her a little shake. 'Don't tell me you're going to give me another lesson in patience. I've got my limits, you know. You're not going to make me wait for marriage, too, are you?'

'No,' she cried happily. 'I've got my own limits.'

'Well, that's all right, then.' He shook his head. 'Why did I have to fall in love with a woman of character?' he asked ruefully.

He kissed her then, and held her to him. As they clung together, Jane could feel a slow warmth steal all along the length of her body where it touched Blake's. She put her arms around his neck, yielding herself up to him, and ran her hands up into the thick black hair.

'I need a bath,' she murmured against his mouth. 'I'm filthy.'

His fingers were busy with the buttons of her blouse. 'I'll help you,' he murmured, spreading the material apart. 'I'm very good at baths. Then later you'll probably want a nap.' Then his hands stilled and he stared down at her. 'You've got it on,' he said.

He reached out and slid one hand over the flesh-coloured teddy that barely covered her breasts. She gasped aloud with sheer pleasure when she felt his fingers graze her bare skin, and when his hand closed over one firm breast, then started gently kneading, she slumped against him weakly.

'Come on,' he murmured hoarsely. 'Let's go have that bath.

HARLEQUIN HISTORICAL

Explore love with Harlequin in the Middle Ages, the Renaissance, in the Regency, the Victorian and other eras.

Relive within these books the endless ages of romance, set against authentic historical backgrounds. Two new historical love stories published each month.

Six exciting series for you every month... from Harlequin

Harlequin Romance·
The series that started it all

Tender, captivating and heartwarming...
love stories that sweep you off to faraway places
and delight you with the magic of love.

◆

Harlequin Presents·

Powerful contemporary love stories...as individual as the women who read them

The No. 1 romance series...
exciting love stories for you, the woman of today...
a rare blend of passion and dramatic realism.

◆

Harlequin Superromance®
It's more than romance...
it's Harlequin Superromance

A sophisticated, contemporary romance-fiction
series, providing you with a longer,
more involving read...a richer mix of complex plots,
realism and adventure.

Harlequin American Romance™
Harlequin celebrates the American woman...

...by offering you romance stories written about American women, by American women for American women. This series offers you contemporary romances uniquely North American in flavor and appeal.

◆

Harlequin Temptation™
Passionate stories for today's woman

An exciting series of sensual, mature stories of love...dilemmas, choices, resolutions... all contemporary issues dealt with in a true-to-life fashion by some of your favorite authors.

◆

Harlequin Intrigue
Because romance can be quite an adventure

Harlequin Intrigue, an innovative series that blends the romance you expect... with the unexpected. Each story has an added element of intrigue that provides a new twist to the Harlequin tradition of romance excellence.

Harlequin Books™

PROD-A-2

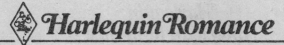# Harlequin Romance

Coming Next Month

Available in March wherever paperback books are sold, or
through Harlequin Reader Service.

In the U.S.
P.O. Box 1397
Buffalo, N.Y.
14240-1397

In Canada
P.O. Box 603
Fort Erie, Ontario
L2A 5X3